W9-CPB-888

PRETTY
PENNY
· FARM ·

PRETTY PENNY FARM

JOANNE HOPPE

Troll Associates

A TROLL BOOK, published by Troll Associates,
Mahwah, NJ 07430

Copyright © 1987 by Joanne Hoppe
Cover copyright © 1987 by Ellen Thompson

All rights reserved. No part of this book may be reproduced or
utilized in any form or by any means, electronic or mechanical,
including photocopying, recording or by any storage and retrieval
system, without permission in writing from the Publisher.

Published by arrangement with William Morrow and Company, Inc.
For information address William Morrow and Company, Inc.,
105 Madison Avenue, New York, New York 10016.

First Troll Printing, 1988

Printed in the United States of America.

10 9 8 7 6 5 4 3 2 1

ISBN 0-8167-1326-X

This book is dedicated to the good memories
of Pretty Penny Farm
and to
Carolyn and John,
who made it possible,
and to
Beth and Lynne and Lisa,
who were there,
and
most especially to
Whitney and Sophie,
whom we will never forget.

 Beth Bridgewater raced out of the house, letting the screen door slam behind her. Her heart was pounding as fast as her feet. Why couldn't her mother just leave her alone? She was fifteen years old and practically in high school, but her mother still treated her like a baby.

And she was so strict! Just thinking about the argument, Beth felt her face tighten again. Everyone else got to go out on weeknights. But not Beth. Oh, no! She'd had to stay home while everyone else went to Amy's party the night before. And this morning her mother had come right out and said she bet Amy's parents weren't even home. Who was she to go around judging everybody else, Beth had shouted. And what if they weren't home? It meant they trusted Amy. That was more than she could say for her mother. Anyway, she'd had the last word. That was something.

It was a gorgeous morning, and Beth's footsteps slowed as the soft summer air began to work on her anger. She stopped to admire a rosebush with enormous, peach-colored blossoms; then she turned the corner and started up the steep hill to Riverdale Junior High School. Only one more week of school. It was exciting to think about high school in the fall, but it was scary. The high school was four times as big as her junior high, and there'd be a whole new drill to learn: Who was in? Who was out? Where to sit? Where not to sit? Who were the good teachers? It had taken at least a year for her to really feel as if she belonged in this school. But now she and Amy and Tory and Darlene— they were the "in" group of ninth graders. So they knew it. What of it? Her mother was always going on about cliques and snobs, but Beth liked belonging, and she wasn't a snob.

She looked up the street. The group was assembled by the big rock in front of the school, their regular meeting place. Like Beth, Darlene and Tory were wearing jeans and T-shirts. Amy, who was already as tan as they would be in midsummer, was flaunting the dress code by wearing a red halter and white shorts. As Beth walked up, Amy did a cartwheel. Kids standing around applauded. Amy was captain of the cheerleaders and the most popular girl in Riverdale, Connecticut. And she's my best friend, Beth thought happily.

"We missed you last night, Beth." Amy swung up to sit on the rock. "It was terrific."

"It was terrific, all right." Tory Barnes pushed back long, blond hair. "I feel like I've been run over by a truck. How will I ever make it through gym class?" She gave an exaggerated groan.

"Hang on to your stomach, blush, and whisper to old lady Barlow that it's that time of the month. She always falls for it," Amy advised. "One month I had my period three times, and she didn't catch on."

They all laughed.

"You should've seen who showed up last night." Darlene grinned at Beth.

"Who?" Beth couldn't help feeling left out, but she tried not to show it.

"I don't know how they found out. You know I said it was going to be just girls. Absolutely no boys allowed." Amy batted her eyelashes in mock innocence.

"Tim Elton and Ken Frey . . ." Darlene began.

"*And* Tony Caputo—what a hunk!" Tory interrupted.

"I couldn't just shut the door in their faces, right?" Amy laughed. "Besides, they brought a couple of six-packs."

Her mother had been right about that, Beth thought. "I'll bet there will be drinking," she had said in that lectury way Beth hated. She probably thought beer stunted your growth.

"I'll never chugalug beer again," Tory vowed.

"You should have seen Tory," Amy said. "She was *so* funny. We're going to have to find some way to get around your mother."

"Yeah. Well . . ." Beth felt uncomfortable. She didn't want to discuss her mother with them. "I've got to go in and study," she said. "I've got a math test first block."

"Don't be a drag, Beth," Amy said. "Besides, it's too late to study now."

Amy was in the same class. "Are you ready?" Beth asked.

"Sure. I'm going to sit next to George Bianchi. He's a brain in math."

"I'd be too afraid to cheat. I'd be afraid I'd get caught," Darlene said.

"Mrs. Wilson is blind as a bat. No sweat." Amy jumped down from the rock. "There comes the bus. My English grade is riding on it."

"What's she talking about?" Darlene asked as Amy ran off toward the bus, which had pulled into the circle in front of the school.

"You know Amy. She's probably conned someone into doing some work for her." Tory sounded envious. "I don't think she's cracked a book all year, and she's always on the honor roll."

Kids spilled off the bus, pushing, jostling, laughing as they jumped down from the high step. Beth and her friends watched as many of them greeted Amy. Most seemed eager to say hello to her. Beth was surprised to see Amy put her arm around the shoulders of a plump, blond girl who smiled happily at the attention.

"Look. She's talking to that obese Sophie Shimmel—whatever." Darlene laughed at the unpronounceable Polish name.

As they watched, Sophie struggled with her notebook, spilling papers to the ground. She knelt down awkwardly to pick them up, handing pages to Amy as she did so.

"What a klutz," Tory said.

Amy waved the papers at them as she crossed the lawn. "Here's my A in English," she said.

"She wrote an essay for you?" Beth asked. "How come? Do you pay her or something?"

"Uh-uh. I just sit with her in class. She doesn't exactly have a lot of friends."

"But she's such a loser," Tory said.

"Listen, she's a good writer." Amy was a little defensive.

"You ought to clue her in," Tory said. "She's a little fat to be walking around without a bra."

"I know why she doesn't wear one. At least, I think I do. She wrote a story about a girl who didn't know how to ask her father if she could buy one."

"Did she read that in class?" Darlene asked. "How embarrassing!"

"She's not that dumb!" Amy retorted. "She marked it 'personal' and got an A+ on it, so I coaxed her until she let me read it."

"Why didn't she ask her mother for a bra?" Beth wanted to know.

"Her mother's dead—at least in the story. The father makes her save all—I mean *all*—her baby-sitting money for college."

"How tacky," Beth said with disgust. "The poor kid

has to walk around with her boobs bouncing."

"That's hysterical, Beth." Amy laughed. She hunched over, sloping her shoulders, pretending to jounce as she moved. " 'Bouncing Boobs' is a good name for her."

"That's not what I meant," Beth protested. "I feel sorry for her."

"Well, sure. So do I. But you have to admit it's funny." Amy continued the imitation.

"Quit that. She's coming over here," Beth whispered.

Sophie Chmielewski, notebook held tightly against her chest and one hand with a paper outstretched, slowly approached. "This is the last page of the *Scarlet Letter* essay," she said to Amy.

"Oh, thanks, Sophie. You're a doll." Amy smiled at her. "That's a really pretty skirt you're wearing."

Sophie looked down at the flowered, flounced skirt.

"It's neat," Tory agreed.

"Where did you get it? New York?" Darlene asked.

Sophie shook her head. She looked uncomfortable. "My aunt sent it to me," she mumbled.

"Your blouse, too?" Amy asked. "I can't really see it with your notebook in the way."

"I've got to go study my math," Beth announced so loudly that the others looked at her in surprise.

"I-have-to-go-too." The words, almost inaudible, came out in one breath as Sophie turned and walked quickly away.

"What's with you, Beth?" Amy demanded.

"I told you. I have to study for the test. I'll see you later." She was uncomfortable as she headed for the building. She felt mean even though she hadn't taken part in the teasing. She didn't understand Amy sometimes. Probably Amy thought that Sophie didn't know they were making fun of her. Even if she didn't, it wasn't right to treat her like some kind of insect they wanted to pin down and see squirm. Well, it was none of Beth's business. And she knew, really, that Amy didn't mean it. She looked at her watch—only ten minutes left until first period. She hurried inside.

The day passed quickly for Beth. The math test was easier than she expected, which was a relief, and in all her other classes the teachers were cramming in everything they hadn't covered during the rest of the year. History was typical. The teacher joked that they had only one week for World War II. The pace was fast, but Beth liked it. She never had time to get bored—not until detention, that is.

It was the first time she had ever been kept after school, and it was going to last all week. Her mother again. The whole group had skipped school the previous Wednesday, but Beth was the only one who had been caught. When the attendance committee had called, everyone else's mother had covered for them. Not hers. Her mother had come right out and said she understood it was ninth grade skip day. So here she was with detention every afternoon while Amy and the rest went to the beach.

It was a long hour, but she managed to get a lot of homework done, so it wasn't a complete loss. Afterward she went to the beach and fooled around. It was after six-thirty when she got home. Her mother would probably get on her case for not being there to help with dinner. She was tired of being the only one who always had to go home early.

"Beth, that you?" her mother called from the living room.

She didn't sound mad. Beth never knew what to expect. Sometimes if they'd had a fight, her mother would barely speak to her. Other times she would act as if nothing had happened.

"Yeah," she called back.

"Come in here, love."

What was going on? Her mother sounded excited.

Her parents were sitting together on the living room couch. They were both smiling as if it were the night before Christmas.

"You're home early, Daddy," Beth said, waiting for an explanation.

"Celebrating." Her father raised a wineglass. "Your mother is going to be rich and famous and get me off the New Haven line."

This was a standing joke. Her mother had tried all sorts of careers. One year she haunted tag sales so she could go into the antique business. Then, always a wonderful cook, she'd taken up catering, and for six months the kitchen had been full of goodies they couldn't eat. That had led to her writing a food column for their local paper, *The Riverdale Gazette*. It had made her well known in their town, but it didn't bring in much money. What now?

"How would you like to spend the summer in New Hampshire?" Elinor Bridgewater beamed at her daughter. Almost unlined at forty-five, she looked particularly young when her dimples showed, as they did now.

"New Hampshire?"

"You know I told you a few weeks ago there was talk that the *Gazette* was going to be picked up by the Granby chain?"

"They sell more newspapers than anyone else in the country," her father said proudly.

"Well, it's happened, and my editor says that my column had a little something to do with it. I don't mean they just bought the paper for my column, but I guess they do like it."

"Don't be modest, El." Charles Bridgewater smiled at his wife. "They're going to carry her column in several of their other publications. She'll be the Dear Abby of the kitchen."

"Oh, Charles, now, not really. But anyway," she said to Beth, "it does mean I'll get a real salary, not just pocket money."

"Mom, that's swell!"

Elinor reached for Beth's hand and pulled her over for a kiss.

"Congratulations, Mom." Beth straightened up. "Now, what's this about New Hampshire?"

"Well, gardening has become a big thing. It's part of this interest in physical fitness and health foods that's been going on a good while. They want the summer columns to combine what you can grow with how you can cook it. So I'm going to have to practice what I write. I'm going to grow a garden."

"In New Hampshire?" Beth didn't get it.

"On Les Helgeson's farm," her father explained. Mr. Helgeson was his partner in the law firm. "He's renting the farm this summer because they're going to Europe and won't be using it until late August. I told your mother about it when she called with the news—"

"And it's perfect," Elinor interrupted. "We don't get enough sun in our backyard, so I would have had to lease land around here anyway. It wouldn't have been easy to find, and it would have been a nuisance commuting to a garden. This way we'll get a summer in the country."

"Also, Mother was thinking of you, Beth. We know how crazy you were about New Hampshire when you went to camp up there."

"But I was ten years old then," Beth said.

"I wouldn't think it's changed much." Her mother looked disappointed.

"Beth, you'll love it," her father said quickly. "It's real country. The farm is on a little dirt road, and the nearest neighbor is half a mile away."

"Is there running water?"

Charles laughed. "Don't worry. There's indoor plumbing and plenty of water for your everlasting hair washing. The Helgesons plan to retire up there, so they've really fixed it up."

"Are you coming, Daddy?"

"With Les away, I'll have to mind the store, but I'll be up on weekends—and maybe I can wangle a week or two."

"Here's a picture, honey," her mother said eagerly. "Alice Helgeson gave it to me today."

The picture showed a large, yellow-shuttered white farmhouse and a big barn.

"It looks great!" Beth exclaimed. "Are there animals in that barn?"

"Their caretaker runs a horse camp not too far from there, and he keeps extra horses at the farm sometimes, I believe," her father said.

"Do you think he'd let me exercise them?" Beth was getting excited about the idea. She'd hate to leave the gang, but if she could ride horses . . . She'd been riding since she was eight and still took lessons. Her big dream was to have a horse. An impossible dream.

"Better than that," her father said. "We'll rent you a horse for the whole summer."

"Charles!" This was obviously news to her mother. "With all the college expenses we have right now?"

"When is Beth ever going to be fifteen and have a chance to spend the summer on a farm with her own horse again? Tomorrow comes very fast. . . ." Her father looked kind of sad. Beth knew he missed her sisters, who were away at school. They'd blown in for a week or two in May and left again . . . Sarah to waitress in Myrtle Beach, and Liza to apprentice at a summer theater on Cape Cod.

Her mother had seen the look, too. "You're right, Charles," she said. She reached out and took Beth's hand. "If there isn't a horse there for you to use, we'll rent you one."

"You mean it?" Beth hugged her mother, then ran to her father. "Daddy, you're neat!" She kissed him. "I've got to call Amy!"

Beth ran into the kitchen and dialed her best friend's number. Amy wasn't home yet, Mrs. Staples told her. Beth was disappointed. It was hard not being able to share something so exciting. Then she had an idea. It would be even more fun going to the country if Amy could go, too. She hurried back into the living room to ask her parents.

"You know, Mom, it's going to be great having a horse and all, but I was thinking . . ."

"What?" Elinor asked.

"Well, it would be really neat if I had someone my own age to hang around with. You know? Would there be room enough for me to invite Amy?"

"Amy?" Her mother's smile disappeared.

"I don't know what you're looking like that for." Beth tried not to sound mad. "She's my best friend, after all."

"I'm not terribly fond of Amy Staples. You know that, Beth."

"I don't know why not. I am." Beth could feel the anger rising.

"I don't trust her, that's why. She's all sweetness and sugar when adults are around, but underneath I think she's a sneaky, mean kid. I'm glad you're going to be away from that whole bunch this summer."

"Now, Elinor"—Charles tried to restore the good mood—"this is no time to lecture Beth about her friends. She's old enough to judge for herself whom she likes. And for your part, Beth, maybe, just for the summer, there'd be someone else you could ask?"

"Wait a minute, Charles." Elinor looked at Beth. "You see, something came up today. I hope it's going to work out all right for everyone. I . . . uh . . ."

"Out with it, Elinor." Charles smiled and shook his head. "You're beating around the bush."

"She's probably just trying to think of some reason why all my friends aren't good enough to invite," Beth snapped.

"That's not true." Elinor was defensive. "I wasn't thinking about your friends. I was thinking it would be nice for you to have another young person up there." She appealed to her husband. "You know I've been over to Gourmet Corners today." Elinor was referring to a store where she had been giving lectures and cooking classes. The manager had frequently given her tips that she had used in her recipes. "The fellow who manages it has been just great to me. He was loading me up with spices and herbs. . . ." She stopped for a minute and licked her lips.

"Well?" Charles prompted.

"He's a widower. With a daughter Beth's age. I think

it's been rough on him . . . and on the girl. He doesn't make a lot of money. He mentioned today he'd never sent her to camp or even taken her on vacation except to visit relatives, so . . ."

"I can see what's coming," Charles said. "You offered to take the kid for the summer." He laughed. "You're always looking after broken wings."

"You mean you've already invited someone up there?" Beth demanded. "Who is this kid, anyway?"

"She's a very nice girl, I'm sure of that," her mother said. "I'm terrible at names, though." She frowned. "I can't think of it, but her father's name is John Chmielewski."

"*What!*" Beth wailed.

"What's wrong, Beth?" Her father put his hand on her shoulder.

"Sophie Chmielewski!" Beth covered her mouth as if she were going to be sick.

"That's right. Her name is Sophie. What's the matter with you, child?" Elinor was shocked at her daughter's reaction.

"She's a creep! Sophie Chmielewski is a fat slob, that's what! Bouncing Boobs! That's her nickname. Bouncing Boobs!" Beth's voice rose higher and louder. "What are you trying to do to me? Everybody makes fun of her. I'll be the laughingstock of the school!"

"Stop screaming this minute," her mother said tersely.

"I can't believe you'd do this." Beth's voice shook with her effort to control it. "You didn't even ask me.

Call her up. Do you hear? Call her up! Tell her she can't go—"

Her father's arm tightened on her shoulders. "Honey, calm down," he said. "Let's just discuss this quietly and rationally."

"Tell *her* that!" Beth glared at her mother. "She's the irrational one. How *dare* she!"

"Don't take that tone with your mother, Beth." He squeezed her shoulder, but his voice was firm.

"I wasn't trying to upset you, Beth. I probably should have asked you, but it all happened so fast. I did think it would be nice for you to have company—"

"Well, you were wrong. I can't," she pleaded. "I can't spend the summer with her...." Beth tried to swallow the sobs that were pushing at her throat. "Call her up. Okay? Call her up and tell her you made a mistake."

Her mother looked close to tears, too. "I can't do that. You know I can't, Beth. It would be too cruel."

"And what you're doing to me isn't cruel?" The injustice of it brought the tears. "Well, take creepy Sophie to New Hampshire. I'm not going!" Beth pulled away from her father and ran sobbing from the room.

"Wait, Beth," she heard him call after her. "Can't we just talk it over?"

She'd never talk to them again. Beth slammed the door to her bedroom and threw herself on the bed, sobbing. She could kill her mother. Sophie Chmielewski! She'd be the joke of the school if she had to spend the summer with her. Well, she'd show them.

Let her mother go to New Hampshire with Sophie. Beth would just stay home and hang around with the gang. She'd smoke and drink and do whatever she wanted to. Let them see how they liked that. She felt as if she would choke with rage and disappointment. She could have had a horse and been on a farm, and her mother had gone and spoiled everything.

"Beth?" Her father was knocking at the door.

"Go away," Beth sobbed.

"Honey, I just want to talk to you for a minute. May I come in?"

Beth didn't answer.

In a few seconds she heard the door open. Her father stood uncertainly in the doorway. "Beth, your mom was wrong," he said. "She meant well. Really she did. But she shouldn't have made those arrangements impulsively without asking you."

He came over and sat on the bed. "Honey, look at me, won't you?" He touched her hair. "I know you're angry, and I don't blame you."

Beth kept her head buried in her arms.

"I know how you feel. Honest. But try to understand your mom. She was elated about the new job and the summer. I think her asking the girl was a way of sharing her good fortune. You know, her excitement just kind of spilled over. Now she's miserable. Everything seems to be ruined."

"Go talk to her!" Beth pounded a fist into the pillow. "She's the one who ruined it!"

"That may be, Beth." He stroked her hair. "But you could help save it."

"You don't understand. I can't go away with that Sophie."

"Why can't you, Beth? Think about it. Is she a terrible person? Does she lie or cheat or hurt other people?"

"I don't know! Don't ask me dumb questions. I don't even know her!" Why couldn't he just go away and leave her alone?

"Then how do you know it wouldn't work?"

Beth pulled away from him and sat up on the far side of the bed, glaring. "You don't understand. You really don't. Just leave me alone, please." She started to cry again and put her hands over her face.

"Honey, I want to help. I want to help you and your mother. I'm going to be honest with you. The main reason your mother wants to go away is because she feels you'll be happy in New Hampshire. She could do her columns here. She's going for you."

"Well, she can just forget it. She doesn't have to do me any favors." Beth choked out the words.

"Let me finish," Charles said quietly. "Neither of us thinks you've been very happy here in quite some time, I guess since your sisters left. We all used to have such a good time together. Now you're angry and sullen more often than you're not."

"At *her*. I'm not that way at school. She still acts like I'm five years old." Beth swung her feet to the floor, her back to her father.

"That may be true. You're our last born. Perhaps we are both guilty of wanting to keep you a child. But we see you and that group of yours wanting to grow up too fast. You're in junior high, Beth, and you're experimenting with things we didn't try until college."

He waited for an answer, but Beth said nothing.

"You're being pulled apart, Beth. We know that. There is one set of values here at home and one in junior high. It's tough. I'd like you to have this summer—this in-between summer—to sort things out for yourself." There was something in his voice that made Beth turn and look at him. His face had the same sad look as when he'd offered to get her that horse. "Be our girl for this one last time before you decide what kind of woman you're going to be."

He held out his arms, and Beth threw her arms around him. There was a certain relief in giving in.

CHAPTER

2

During the drive to New Hampshire, Beth insisted on sitting alone in the backseat pretending to be absorbed in a book. Her mother was stuck. She couldn't make Beth talk. Mile after mile she and Sophie made halting conversation while Beth sulked. Several times Sophie offered her cookies and pastries Mr. Chmielewski had made for the trip. They looked delicious, but Beth would have starved before accepting one.

They had stopped at a gas station for a Coke, and her mother had followed her into the ladies' room. "Can't you please make a little bit of an effort?" her mother pleaded.

"I promised Daddy I would come up here for two weeks and try it, but that's all I promised," Beth shot back.

"Sophie's such a shy girl. I feel sorry for her," her mother said.

"I think she's gross," Beth said, slamming out of the room.

"You're making it very difficult," her mother whispered behind her.

Difficult, Beth thought, settling into the backseat again. What about how difficult it had been for her this past week? Her group had been merciless once they found out. She grimaced, remembering the scene in the lunchroom the last day.

After their English class, Amy had come up with Sophie. "I thought Beth and Sophie ought to get to know each other better," she announced, "so Sophie's going to sit at our table today. Right, Sophie?"

Sophie blushed and smiled.

"Here, Sophie, I'll move over so you can sit next to Beth," Tory said, giggling.

Sophie awkwardly tried to squeeze into the small space Tory had made on the bench. "Oops." Tory pretended to fall off the end. "I guess there isn't room for both of us. I'll sit over here." She moved to the other side of the table.

Beth pushed her tray of spaghetti away.

"Aren't you hungry, Beth?" Amy asked. "Maybe Sophie would like some. How about a real Italian lunch? Have some spaghetti with your pizza?" She held up Beth's plate.

Sophie shook her head. She pushed the pizza around on her plate.

"Sophie's not hungry either?" Tory said. "You two have a lot in common."

"Knock it off, Tory," Beth warned.

"Tory's just fooling around," Amy said.

"I don't like to be laughed at." Beth was defiant.

"Come on. We're not laughing at anyone." Amy winked at her. "Besides, I don't think you and Sophie are a bit alike, but *vive la différence*. Right, Sophie?"

Sophie shrugged, then nodded. Her face was flushed.

"Sophie has it all over you in the boobs department," Amy went on.

Sophie sat slumped on the bench as if her shoulders could cover her breasts. Now she crossed her arms over them. Beth could see the sweat on her forehead.

I'm sorry for her, she thought desperately, but I won't be lumped with her. "I'm a late bloomer, I guess," she said, "but Sophie's already blossomed."

Everyone but Sophie had laughed. Beth felt secure. Why, then, did she have such a knot in her stomach?

Turning it over in her mind again, she resolutely pushed down the guilt. Why should she feel ashamed? Sophie was the creep, not her.

Her thoughts were interrupted by her mother's announcing they had arrived at their exit. She put down the book and looked out the window.

They had turned off onto a main road. There were some farms, but many of the buildings were single houses. A few had signs that announced "Antiques." Most of them seemed freshly painted and well kept, but an occasional house had grayed and sagged under the weight of New England winters. Elinor stopped at a roadside stand and bought lettuce, honey, and fresh eggs.

They reached the center of town. There was a market, a gas station, a general store that also housed the barbershop, a drugstore, the town hall, and a diner. A little farther on was the firehouse. Just past it was a tarred road. The street marker read "Pumpkin Hill Road." Below this, a sign reading "Fuller's Horse Camp" pointed up the steep hill.

"We have to stop at Fuller's and pick up the keys," Elinor said, as she made an almost perpendicular right by the sign.

Near the town the houses had been close together, but farther up Pumpkin Hill they thinned out. On the left were fields enclosed by split-rail fencing where horses were grazing. Up ahead they could see a group of buildings across from a large barn.

There was a place to pull off in front of a long low building that looked like a barracks. Next to it stood a smallish house. All of the structures were painted a dark red except for the weathered barn. Several girls who looked anywhere from eight to sixteen came out of the barracks and headed for the house.

Elinor got out of the car, and Beth quickly opened the back door. She was glad to get out and stretch. A boy about thirteen or so with sun-streaked blond hair came through the screened door of the house.

"Lunch is on. Come on in." He waved to the group

of girls. Then he walked over to Beth and her mother.

"Hi. Could you tell me where I might find Mr. Fuller?" Elinor smiled at him.

"He's not home right now," the boy answered. "I'm his son Jack. My ma's inside getting on the lunch. You a new camper?" he asked Beth.

She shook her head no.

"We're staying at the Helgesons' for the summer. Your dad has the key, I believe," Elinor explained.

"Sure thing," Jack said. "You hold on a minute, and I'll get it."

"I'm going to take a look around," Beth said. She walked past the barracks to where there was a fenced-in field. Obviously the lessons were given here, and maybe shows. Jumps were set up, and a small set of bleachers was placed on each side. No one was working out at the moment, probably because it was meal-time.

She started across the street to see if there were any horses in the barn, but heard her mother calling that she was ready to go.

"Something sure smells good around here," her mother was saying to Sophie as Beth got in.

"Honeysuckle," Sophie said. "I don't see it, but there's plenty here somewhere."

"I believe you're right," Elinor agreed.

It was a heavy, sweet scent. Almost too flowery, Beth thought. She liked better the sweet smell of the grasses and the rich smell of manure.

"It's not far from here," Elinor said. "First we'll see a

little graveyard; then the farm will be half a mile beyond it on the left."

They had just passed the graveyard when Sophie gasped, "Oh, look! Look quick! On the tree."

Elinor slammed on the brakes, jolting Beth. "What is it?" she asked.

"Mushrooms. See?" Sophie pointed to a clump on a leafless tree. It was off-white and looked like a shelf. "They are really good ones!" Sophie was very excited.

"I don't know a thing about wild mushrooms," Elinor said, "but that looks like a fungus to me."

"They are good. Honest. They are called oyster mushrooms, but they taste a lot like chicken. Do you have a knife?" Sophie asked.

"No, but there'll be one at the farm." Elinor accelerated slowly. "We can come back later. I have to tell you, though; I don't think I want to take a chance eating wild mushrooms."

"I brought my mushroom guide. I can show them to you. Besides, you don't have to worry. No fungus that grows on a tree is poisonous," Sophie told her.

"It sounds as if you're a mycologist," Elinor said. "That's an expert in mushrooms," she explained to Beth.

"I'm not really an expert, but my father is. He's been teaching me about them since I can remember."

It was the first time Beth had ever seen Sophie show any real life, in or out of school. And it was over some dumb growth on a tree. She couldn't figure it.

"It would be fun to do a column about mushrooms.

You'll have to help me, Sophie." Elinor was enthusiastic. "I'll bet people would be really interested. What do you think, Beth?"

"Uh-huh," Beth grunted, looking out the window for her first sight of the farm.

"Look!" Elinor pointed to the top of the hill. "That's got to be it."

The farmhouse was beautiful. White, with yellow shutters, it sat nestled against the brow of a hill overlooking a gently sloping meadow studded with apple trees and bordered by a grape arbor. Baskets of impatiens were fastened on one side of the large rolling door of the beautifully weathered barn. Just below the buildings and the meadow was a small pond.

The sign by the driveway said "Pretty Penny Farm." "That's a funny name," Sophie said.

"The Helgesons paid a pretty penny for it. That's where the name comes from," Elinor explained as she pulled in and parked.

The car had hardly stopped before Beth was out of it and headed for the barn. "I'm going to see if there are any horses," she called over her shoulder.

Beth grasped the wooden handle of the barn door. It was heavy, and she had to put her shoulder to it to roll the door back. Inside, the barn smelled of hay and manure. The large center of the barn was open to the roof. On either side were haymows. A ladder leaned against the one to her left. Below it, on the floor, were grain bins and pails, and on the wall tools were hung, and what looked to be some old tack.

There was a door to her right. Beth opened it and found herself in a long, narrow room lined with stanchions for cows. They were rusty— obviously not used recently. She went back into the main part of the barn. Toward the rear, on her left, she found a box stall and two smaller horse stalls. There was fresh sawdust on the floor, and a grain bucket with a sprinkling of oats. The stalls were empty. She came out and opened a door in the center of the rear wall. Beth found herself in a pretty lane, bordered by grassy meadows on either side of the split-rail fences. She walked about a quarter of a mile until it led into a small, enclosed pasture. Beyond it she could see a larger pasture. The gate to the small pasture stood half open, and Beth leaned on it looking at the two horses who were gazing at her.

The taller one, a handsome chestnut with a white blaze on his forehead, ears pointed, eyed her curiously. The smaller horse, a bay mare with a cropped, bristled mane, trotted past the chestnut and came straight to Beth.

"What a cute thing you are!" Beth rubbed the mare's nose and scratched her ears, but she was watching the chestnut. His head was high, his eyes alert. Suddenly he broke into a run. Close to the fence, he circled the little pasture. Hooves thudding, mane flying, he looked like Beth's dream of the perfect horse—spirited and free. "Oh, how I'd love to ride you," she said out loud.

As if he had understood her, the chestnut slowed from a gallop to a canter, then stopped a few feet away. Tossing his head, he came closer, and the mare moved off. "I see who's boss around here," Beth said, reaching out and gently stroking his nose. The chestnut pulled back, then put his head down toward her hand. "I'm sorry. I don't have any treats." She put out her hand, flat, palm side up, to show him. "See." He sniffed the palm, then tossed his head. "I'll go get you some sugar," Beth promised.

"Beth!" It was her mother, coming down the lane with a tall man. As they drew closer, she saw that the man was very tan, with deep wrinkles around his eyes and mouth. Dark, wavy hair was shot with gray at the left temple and above his ears. His eyes were blue and friendly.

"This is Mr. Fuller," her mother introduced him.

"I love these horses," Beth said as the little mare trotted over. "Are they yours?"

"Ayeh." Percy Fuller used the New Hampshire version of "yes." "Dolly heah is a little pet. She'd foller you into the house if you'd let her." He slapped the mare's neck affectionately. "She's about as friendly as a kitten."

"That's a beautiful horse." Beth pointed to the chestnut.

"Charmin'? Ayeh. He's right nice-lookin', but he's a mite skittish. High-strung. Not good for camp."

"Charmin'. What a great name," Beth said. "Come here, Charmin'. Come here, boy." She pulled open the gate and walked toward him, slowly and quietly, being careful not to startle him. He eyed her curiously, seeming to be sizing her up. Her outstretched hand was almost touching him when he tossed his head and ran a few feet away. Then he turned to see what she would do. "You're just a tease, Charmin'. You're playing games with me," she said after he repeated the maneuver several times. Beth turned and walked back to the others. She smiled at Mr. Fuller. "I would love to ride him," she said.

"You'd have to catch him first," Mr. Fuller teased.

Beth was about to respond when a boy in sweats came running toward them. He stopped abruptly, looking from Beth and her mother to Mr. Fuller.

"My son Dave," Mr. Fuller introduced him. "These are the Bridgewaters—going to be spending the summer. Beth heah seems to have taken quite a fancy to Charmin'. It's Dave's hoss," he explained.

Dave frowned, and Beth felt her hopes diminish.

"Won him on a bet at school." Mr. Fuller did not sound too pleased. "Don't hold much with fancy schools where folks go round bettin' on Thoroughbred hosses. Still don't know what you could have put up."

"It doesn't matter, does it? I didn't lose." Dave Fuller sounded as if they'd had this discussion before.

"Where do you go to school?" Elinor asked.

"University of Virginia," Dave answered.

"Got himself a track scholarship down there." Percy Fuller's lips tightened. "Could have gone to our own state university—"

"Not on a full scholarship, Dad." Dave nodded to Elinor Bridgewater. "Nice to meet you."

"Well, looka that." Percy Fuller grinned. "'Pears

like Charmin's taken a shine to Beth." The horse had come over and nudged Beth's shoulder. "That's not like him to be so friendly, is it, Dave?"

Dave, who had started to run off, turned back. Delighted, Beth reached her hand up and stroked the horse's neck. "You are the most beautiful horse I've ever seen," she whispered.

"You say Charmin' is headstrong?" Elinor asked.

"He knows his own mind. That's for sure," Percy replied.

"You see . . ." Elinor hesitated. "We're looking for a horse to rent. We want Beth to have her own horse for the summer. But it has to be a safe horse."

"Then you don't want Charmin'," Dave said to her quickly. "He's no tame saddle horse."

"I can handle horses," Beth said. "I don't need some old plug that doesn't go above a trot."

"Of course you don't, honey," Elinor said. "I just meant we don't want a wild, difficult horse."

"That's just what he is," Dave said. "What about Dolly, Dad? She'd be a good horse for her. Or are you going to use her at camp?"

"No. I could spare her. Dolly heah would be perfect for you," Mr. Fuller said to Beth.

"No!" Beth hadn't meant to sound so vehement. "I mean, she's adorable, but I—" She stopped and looked at Dave. "Charmin's just the kind of horse I've always wanted. But I guess you don't want someone else riding your horse. I can understand that."

"He only rides when he has to," Mr. Fuller answered

for Dave. "Doesn't enjoy it the way he used to 'fore he went off to school." He ignored Dave's scowl. "Still, that's an awful lot of hoss for a little girl."

"I'm almost five-five." Beth straightened up, standing as tall as she could. "I've been riding since I was eight years old."

"Honey, what's wrong with the mare?" Elinor asked. "She's such a sweet thing, and I'm sure she would be a good ride, but a safe one."

"You don't know anything about horses, Mother. No offense, but I do. I'm sure I could handle Charmin'." She looked at Dave. "If he's available."

"Maybe there's a horse at camp she'd like," Dave suggested, ignoring her question.

"Nope. I'm running at capacity right now," his father replied. "Tell you what"—he smiled at Beth—"I don't think Charmin's as bad as Dave here makes out. We'll have a little tryout here—take a look at your riding and see what's what. Fair enough?"

Beth could have hugged him. "You mean I can ride him now?" she asked.

"If it's all right with your mother."

"Well, I . . ." Elinor looked worried.

"Please, Mom? I'll be careful, honest. Please?" Beth pleaded.

Elinor nodded, but Beth could see the concern in her eyes. She squeezed her mother's arm. "Thanks, Mom. It'll be okay. You'll see."

Mr. Fuller led Charmin' up to the barn, and Dolly tagged along behind. He put the chestnut on crossties and Beth brushed him before she put on the tack. Mr. Fuller nodded at her approvingly, and let her lead Charmin' out of the barn. She noticed Dave had stayed to watch the test.

Charmin' was tall, and Beth could barely get her foot in the stirrup to mount. The horse danced around, and Dave started forward to hold him, but Beth insisted on managing by herself. She wasn't going to give them any reason to say she couldn't handle Charmin'. Her hands were trembling from excitement, and also, she had to admit to herself, a little bit of fear.

Charmin' responded immediately to the slight pressure of her knees and broke into a trot. They trotted up through the meadow. It was on a gradual incline that peaked and fell off more sharply on the far side. Beth urged Charmin' into a canter. His gait was incredibly smooth, she thought.

Suddenly the chestnut lunged forward. Beth tried to check him, but he galloped over the crest of the hill and down the steep decline. Feeling that she might fly over his head at any moment, she gripped tightly with her knees and hunched forward. The reins hurt Beth's hands as she pulled back with all her strength. Charmin's pace did not slacken. There was a tree directly ahead with low branches. She would certainly be knocked off! Charmin' swerved, and Beth slipped to one side and hung there. She looked at the ground moving rapidly under her and wanted to cry. She bit her lip and grabbed for the horse's mane, trying desperately to regain the stirrup with her right foot. It was in! She had her seat again. She slipped the left foot into the stirrup. "Darn you, Charmin'," she scolded as she yanked on the left rein, taking him in a wide circle. His speed lessened, and Beth put pressure on the reins until he fell back to a canter. Looking at the hill they had to go back up, Beth decided to take him on a diagonal. "No more bolting for you," she said. They reached the crest and came down to a trot heading back to the barn.

" 'Pears like you managed him," Mr. Fuller said when she reined in.

Good thing they hadn't seen her at the other end of the meadow, Beth thought. "He's great!" she told them breathlessly.

"Worked up a bit of a lather, though, didn't you?" Percy Fuller fingered the dark stain outlining the saddle.

"I let him have his head. Wanted to see what he could do," Beth fibbed.

He looked her directly in the eye. "That right?"

Beth blushed. "I'll work with him. I can handle him."

"I don't like it, Dad." Dave Fuller was frowning, and Beth thought she was going to lose her chance. She wanted Charmin' so much!

"I'll take good care of him," she pleaded.

"Hoss has to earn his keep, Dave," Mr. Fuller said. "Besides, he needs to be ridden, and you don't keep up your end of that."

"I'll ride him every day," Beth promised.

"You'd have to sign a form taking the responsibility, Miz Bridgewater," Percy said.

"You'd sign, wouldn't you, Mom?" Beth's eyes begged.

Elinor looked from one to the other and hesitated. Beth held her breath.

"It has to be this horse, Beth?" Elinor shook her head worriedly.

"Mom, it'll be the best summer of my life if I can use Charmin'," Beth answered.

"You're sure you can handle him?"

"I swear it!"

"We'll take the responsibility, Mr. Fuller," Elinor said slowly.

"I wouldn't want you taking him far." Dave did not look pleased with the arrangement. "It would be better if you rode him around here." Seeing Beth's puzzled look, he continued, "If you have any trouble with him, you're close to home."

"Well, looks like you've got yourself a hoss for the summer, Beth." Percy smiled. "Better walk him around and cool him down once you take the saddle off."

Sophie appeared from the side of the barn. "What about your sister heah"—he gestured at the girl—"is she going to want to ride, too?"

"She's not my sister." Beth jerked on the girth to unloosen the saddle.

"This is Sophie Chmielewski," Elinor said quickly. "A friend who's spending the summer with us. Sophie, meet Mr. Fuller and his son Dave."

"Hello," she said shyly.

"Do you ride, Sophie?" Elinor asked.

Sophie's eyes were wide as she looked at the large chestnut. She shook her head.

"Dave, go bring up Dolly. Doesn't seem right for one young'un to have a hoss and not the other," Mr. Fuller said.

"We'd better talk a little about the terms, Mr. Fuller," Elinor said quickly. "What are your rates for renting the horses?"

"We-ell . . ." Percy Fuller considered. "The girls could do the feedin' and waterin' . . . save me time comin' up heah. Then I was goin' to hire an extra hand at camp. Maybe they could each work 'bout ten hours a week? Seem fair?"

"More than fair." Elinor was relieved. "Beth?"

"That's great. I love being around horses. I'll be glad to work!" She gave Charmin' an affectionate pat as she walked him around.

"How does that sound to you, Sophie?" Elinor put her hand on the girl's shoulder. "Would you like to have your own horse for the summer?"

Sophie hung her head, embarrassed. "I'm afraid of horses." Her voice was almost a whisper.

"Not this one." Mr. Fuller pointed at Dolly. Dave Fuller took the bars down and brought her out of the lane. "Go up and get acquainted," Mr. Fuller urged.

Sophie hung back. "Go on now," he coaxed. Sophie hesitated. She looked at Dolly and took a couple of slow steps forward. Dolly rolled back her upper lip and stretched toward Sophie's shoulder. Sophie gasped and jumped back. "She's going to bite me."

"Not on your life." Mr. Fuller laughed. "See!" He walked up to Dolly, whose curled-back lips revealed enormous teeth. The mare ran her muzzle over his upper arm. "She wanted to give you a kiss. She's a lovin' little animal. Come heah, now."

Sophie moved close to Mr. Fuller, who was talking softly to Dolly. "Don't you scare her no more," he said. "Show the little girl how nice y'are. Just put up your hand, Sophie, and scratch her behind the ear," he directed.

Sophie reached up, and Dolly responded by nuzzling her in the stomach. She pulled back, but Mr. Fuller said, "See. She likes you."

"Oh, she's sweet!" Sophie sounded pleased.

"You come along, then, and I'll show you how ta put on a saddle." Percy Fuller winked at Elinor. "We'll turn her into a hosswoman 'fore the summah's over," he said.

Beth finished cooling down Charmin' and put him back in the lane. Mr. Fuller led Dolly out of the barn just as Beth got there.

"Could I see Beth ride her first?" Sophie asked.

"Sure," Mr. Fuller said. "Show her how easy she goes, Beth."

After Charmin', riding Dolly was as simple as riding a rocking horse, Beth thought. In fact, the mare's bouncy little gaits gave her just that feeling.

"She's a lamb," Beth said, riding up to Sophie.

"Here. You try her." She slid off the mare and held on to the bridle.

Sophie moved slowly up to the right side of the horse.

"Other side," said Beth. Couldn't this dippy girl do anything?

"Fust time on a hoss, everyone's scared," Percy Fuller encouraged. "I'll help ya up."

Sophie slid her foot into the stirrup.

"Hold on to the front of the saddle and pull," Mr. Fuller said.

Sophie tried, but slid back down. The next time he gave her a boost, and she got her leg across the saddle.

"There you are!" Percy smiled.

"Thanks, Mr. Fuller." Sophie grinned happily.

Heehaw. Heehaw. Heehaw. The loud noise of a horn from the driveway startled the little mare, who lunged forward, throwing Beth off balance. The bridle was jerked from her hands.

"*Help!*" Sophie yelled as Dolly bolted. Sophie grabbed at Dolly's mane, but was knocked to the ground.

Dave broke into a run. Dolly had slowed down almost immediately, and he had no trouble catching her rein. "Whoa, whoa," he ordered, pulling hard. "Okay, girl, okay," he soothed, calming the startled horse.

"Are you all right?" Elinor was kneeling by Sophie, who was facedown in the grass. She pushed herself up to a crouch and looked at her hands, which were scraped.

"Do ya hurt anywhere?" Mr. Fuller knelt down.

"All over." Sophie was fighting tears, but one rolled down her cheek, mixing with the dirt smudged there.

"Sure. You've had the wind knocked out of ya." He lifted her arm gingerly and put it over his shoulder. "Let's see if you can stand up," he said.

Elinor took Sophie's other arm, and slowly they helped her stand. "Everything seems to be movin' all right," Mr. Fuller said as they walked her around.

"I'm sorry." Sophie bit her lip. "I didn't mean to cause so much trouble."

"You didn't. It was that durned fool with his asinine horn. Wait till I see—" Mr. Fuller stopped as a short boy with straw-colored hair came around the barn. "Well, speak of the devil. Clammy Ellis!" he addressed the youth. "You must have been somewhere else when the good Lord was handin' out brains."

"Huh? What you talking about?" Clammy scratched his head, his brown eyes puzzled.

"You—honking that donkey horn of yours. You spooked the hoss and she"—he motioned at Sophie— "fell off. Coulda hurt herself."

"Hey. I'm sorry." He came over to Sophie. "I didn't know anyone was riding back here. You all right?"

"She's gonna smart for a few days." Percy's face was stern. "Think you'd know better'n to drive around blasting that ungodly noisemaker."

"I'll get rid of it, Percy. Honest," Clammy declared. "It's not worth getting worked up about."

"What are you doing here, anyway?" Percy's face

relaxed a little. "I thought you were working Josie's Babe."

"I was, but I came to find you. See what you'd think if I took her over to the track at the fairground. There's too much going on at camp and I think it's time to get her over there."

"Might be. Take the small trailer," Percy said.

"Dad's got a filly he's going to race at the Warrington County Fair in August," Dave explained.

"And this is Clammy Ellis." Percy Fuller performed belated introductions. "If he shows more sense in the next month than he did today, he'll be riding her."

"I'll be riding her." Clammy grinned. "Josie's Babe is going to win that race."

CHAPTER 3

Charles Bridgewater came up the following weekend, and on Saturday night they went to a square dance at the local Grange. A white clapboard building, it contained an entry hall with hooks for coats, and one large main room with a tiny stage and chairs lining three walls. A refreshment table was set up in the far end of the room where a door led to a small kitchen.

A fiddler was tuning up on the stage, and a plump, gray-haired lady with glasses was seated at a piano to his left. On the other side of the stage, Clammy Ellis and a round-faced, laughing man in overalls were setting up a microphone.

"Testing. One. Two. Three." The man's voice boomed.

At this, Clammy, apparently satisfied that the microphone worked, waved his hand and jumped off the stage.

Beth looked around the room. She was hoping to see Dave Fuller. He was so good-looking with his curly brown hair and big brown eyes. She couldn't remember ever having paid much attention to a boy's eyes before, but Dave had thick, black lashes that were, well, sexy. He also had a great build, probably from running. He wasn't muscly in the way some of the jocks at home were, but there wasn't an ounce of flab on him. He had the perfect body for blue jean commercials, she decided.

There were a lot of people, some sitting in the chairs along the walls, other clustered in groups, standing. She didn't see the Fullers anywhere.

"Choose your partners!" The man in overalls on the stage was obviously the caller, and he announced the first square dance.

"Want to try it?" Charles Bridgewater asked his wife.

"I haven't square-danced in years," she protested. "Let's watch awhile first."

They found seats by the wall. "Come on! Don't be bashful! Get a partner and get on the floor!" The caller clapped his hands. "Ye-ow! Let's go, fellas and gals!"

"Hi there, folks." Clammy Ellis came up to them. "How you doing? You get over your spill?"

Sophie blushed and nodded.

"How 'bout a dance to show there are no hard feelings?" Clammy motioned to the floor.

The red in Sophie's face deepened, but she got to her feet. "Okay," she said.

Sophie was wearing a flowered cotton skirt and a smocked blouse. It was the kind of outfit that set her apart from the alligator-shirted, blue-jeaned crowd at home, but here it seemed to fit right in. Most of the girls were in full dresses or skirts. Only Beth and some of the campers from Fuller's were in the uniform of the sophisticated suburbs.

There was much laughter as the girls and women lined up across from the men. "Groups of four," the caller commanded. There was shuffling up and down the line as quartets counted off. "Need another couple right there on the end. Come on, folks, one more couple," the caller coaxed.

"How about it? Want to dance?" Beth turned in surprise. She had been so intent watching the floor, she hadn't seen Dave Fuller come up.

"I've never square-danced." She spread her hands helplessly.

"It's easy." Dave pulled her to her feet. "Just do what the caller says." He led her along, laughing, to the very end of the line.

"Thank you, Dave." The caller waved to them. "All right, everybody, honor your partner." Dave bowed to Beth, and she started to bow back until she realized the other girls were curtsying. She quickly corrected herself.

"Now, honor your connah." What was a "connah," Beth wondered, at first not understanding the New

Hampshire pronunciation of "corner."

The man to her right smiled and bowed as Dave bowed to the girl on his left. This time she knew enough to curtsy.

"Now, swing your partner, do-si-do."

Da-dum-dum-da, da-dum-dum-da, da-dum-dum-da, da-da-dum-dum-da," went the fiddle as Dave, his arm tight around her waist, swung her around first one way, then the other.

"Now, swing your connah!"

Beth and the other girl skipped to the center at the same time and collided. The other girl laughed, but Beth felt like a fool.

"No. No. She goes first," Dave explained.

Beth retreated as Dave and the girl spun around.

"Now you," Dave said, pointing, and Beth and her corner linked arms and twirled.

"Form a star." The other three couples stretched out their left arms until their fingers touched.

"Come on, Beth!" Dave called. She raised her arm tentatively, and they circled, hands touching, in rhythm with the music.

"Allemande left and allemande right. Do it the first time, and do it *right!*" The caller was speeding up the tempo, and the fiddle obeyed.

"Swing your partner, do-si-do; don't step on that pretty little toe."

Out of the corner of her eye, Beth caught sight of Sophie twirling gracefully and laughing.

"Promenade!" They marched in couples.

"Ladies' chain."

Beth came abreast of Sophie. "Isn't this fun, Beth?" Sophie's eyes were shining.

"Grand right and left!"

Beth would barely get the steps to one call before the next call came, and all the time the music went faster and faster.

"Swing her high and swing her low! That's all there is; there isn't any mo'!"

Beth lost her balance on the last mad swing, and Dave kept her from falling to the floor. She was out of breath from laughing and dancing, and he kept an arm around her as they headed for the seats.

"Hey, that looked like fun," her father said.

"Let me fix your ribbon," her mother offered. Beth had tied her long dark brown hair back, but in the heat of the dance the ribbon had slipped and now dangled, nearly off. Her hair hung loose around her face and shoulders.

"I'll fix it in a minute," she said, pulling off the ribbon.

"Catch your breath, and we'll get a drink," Dave offered. Beth was relieved. He wasn't going to dance with her once and then dump her.

"Sophie, you're good!" her mother exclaimed as Sophie and Clammy came up and collapsed into chairs.

"You're better'n any of the girls around here," Clammy said. "Where'd you learn?"

"I didn't learn this, but my father—and my aunts in Buffalo—they know all the old folk dances, from Poland. I've been doing them since I was a little kid. They're not so different from your square dance." Sophie, flushed and smiling, spoke with unusual animation.

She could really be pretty. Beth was surprised at the thought. Some blond hair had escaped from the tight braids Sophie always wore, and it looked soft and shiny around her face. She had beautiful skin, not a zit to be seen. But she was just too fat.

"You're so graceful," Elinor said. "I noticed how beautifully you used your hands. Are they traditional gestures, too?"

Sophie nodded, beaming.

But she was such a klutz at school, Beth thought. Like some poor panting fish on the beach.

The music was starting again. "Let's wait until after this set to have a drink," Dave said. "I want to dance with Sophie."

Beth felt her jaw start to go slack, but she quickly recovered. "Sure," she said.

"Do you want to dance?" Clammy offered as Dave and Sophie went out on the floor.

"No thanks," Beth answered. "I'm not very good, and I haven't got my breath from the last one." Not as good as Sophie anyway. The idea rankled.

Her mother and father joined the couples on the floor, and Clammy moved next to her to watch the dancing. This was different from dances at home. There were kids out there who couldn't have been more than seven or eight and people in their seventies.

There was every age in between. Beth had to admit Sophie was one of the best dancers on the floor. She kept in perfect step and made it all look easy. Beth could have died, thinking of all the dumb mistakes she'd made. Was she jealous of Sophie? Of course not—that would be ridiculous.

"How do you like that chestnut of Dave's you hired?" Clammy asked.

"He's fantastic." Beth launched into her favorite subject. "He's so strong, you know? And fast. I've never been on a horse like him."

"Kinda ornery, though, isn't he?" Clammy asked.

"No. I mean he'd like to be boss, I guess, but it's such a great feeling to argue with him and win. And he's so charmin', just like his name. Already he knows my footsteps, and if he hears me in the barn, he comes and raps on the back door with his hoof. Actually, Daddy wasn't too thrilled when he saw the marks on the door, but I think it's adorable."

"If you like horses, you ought to come watch Josie's Babe work out at the fairgrounds some morning."

"That's Mr. Fuller's horse that you're going to race?" Beth asked.

"Yup. This is my second race. Percy Fuller's the one who started me thinking about being a jockey. I've worked at his camp in the summers. Always hated being short and skinny till he started me thinking about racing."

"You're not all that short," Beth said. "How old are you anyway?"

"Seventeen. And five-four ain't real tall. But with my weight, it's good for a jock. My pop doesn't think much of the idea, but if I win this race, I think he might let me go off and train proper."

"Why is this race so important?" Beth asked. "Couldn't you enter others?"

"Well, you see, it's kinda the tradition. This is the biggest purse of the county fair meet—ten thousand dollars—and any local farmers or horsemen who think they got a good horse try it out in this race. If they come in in the money, then sure, they take them to other races, to regular tracks."

"What are your chances of winning?" Beth asked.

"I dunno. Josie's Babe is a nice steady filly. She's looking better every day. I think we've got as good a chance as any, but no horse race is ever a sure thing."

The dance ended, and Sophie and Dave came back. "You guys ready for a drink?" Dave asked.

"Not with that music playing." Clammy got to his feet. "Can you do another one?" he asked Sophie.

"She'll die of thirst, Clammy," Dave said.

"No. No. I love to dance. I can have a drink later." Sophie was heaving.

"See you," Dave said, and guided Beth to the refreshment table. "You got a big choice. Coke or apple cider. I imagine you're too young for anything else anyway, aren't you?"

Beth felt her face go warm. "I'm not *so* young," she retorted. "How old are you anyway?"

"Almost nineteen," he told her. "What about you?"

"Almost sixteen," she lied. She had just turned fifteen in May.

"Hardly legal." The way he smiled at her made her feel funny.

"I'll have cider," she said.

"And a doughnut? You want to do the country scene?" he asked.

"What do you mean?"

"You probably find this pretty much of a hick town, don't you? Square dances, cider, doughnuts. Ayeh, you prob'ly think it's kinda quaint." He exaggerated the New Hampshire accent. Beth hadn't noticed until then that there was usually very little trace of it in Dave's speech.

"I don't think about it that way at all." Beth said. "I love it here. The farm is great, and Charmin' . . . I'm just having the best time."

"It can get pretty dull here, you'll find." Dave handed her a paper cup of cider.

"You like Virginia better?" Beth asked.

Dave didn't answer right away.

"I hear it's a great school."

"It's a big party school," he said.

"That must be fun."

He shrugged. "Yes and no. Anyway, as I was saying, the quiet here is deafening."

"Then why did you come home for the summer?" Beth felt a little annoyed at his criticism of the place she was learning to love.

"The old man needs me," Dave answered. "The

camp is a two-bit operation, and he can't afford to hire much help. He depends on me and my brother, Jack. Besides, I had to bring the horse up."

"Am I glad you did," Beth said. "It's hard to believe you won him on a bet. What luck!" She wished it had happened to her.

"Yup." He changed the subject. "Want to walk outside and cool off?"

"Sure."

Dave touched her arm and steered her toward the front door. "I can't imagine anyone willing to bet Charmin'," Beth said.

"My roommate was. His family has horses coming out their ears," he explained. "What a setup they've got. A big old southern mansion. You know—with the long tree-lined driveway. And two sets of stables. It's hunt and racing country."

"So that's why Charmin' is so fast."

"He's no racehorse," Dave said quickly. "They've got horses down there that would make him look like a plow horse. Hey"—he pointed out a couple sitting on a bench in front of the building—"looks like Clammy finally let your friend have a rest."

She's not my friend, Beth wanted to say, but she kept quiet.

"Bending her ear about the race?" Dave asked Clammy.

"It sounds really exciting." Sophie smiled.

"Might be if he had a chance," Dave answered.

"You going to start that business again about races being fixed, Dave?" Clammy asked.

"Lots of them are," he replied. "Besides, I think you're bucking odds, riding against pros. They're not going to let you country boys get anywhere near that finish line."

"That's not what your pa says." There was an edge to Clammy's voice.

"What does he know about racing? Don't get me wrong. I'd like to see you win. I just don't like to see the two of you counting on it."

"You become some kind of authority because you're a college boy?" Clammy was testy.

"Come off of it, Clammy. You know better than that."

"Do I? What I know is that we're going to give it the old run for the money." He got up from the bench. "Music's started," he said to Sophie. "Want to dance?"

"Can't tell them anything," Dave said, once the others had left. "And I'm really getting sick of this think-you're-smart-college-kid stuff. Well, I did learn a few things last year."

Beth knew just how he felt.

"I've got to be going," he said abruptly. "See you."

Beth stood staring after him. He had been so friendly, had seemed to like her. Why had he taken off like that?

CHAPTER 4

Beth was awakened early the next morning by the sunlight coming in her windows. She loved waking up in this bedroom with its old-fashioned white ruffled curtains and cheery rose-patterned wallpaper. She propped herself up on the pillows and looked at the alarm clock on the pine nightstand next to her bed. It was only six-thirty. The house was quiet, the rest of its occupants still asleep. She liked that. It was special, not at all lonely, having these early hours to herself.

The floors were oak and highly polished, and when she stepped off the scatter rug by her bed, they felt cool under her bare feet.

She opened her bedroom door quietly, careful not to make noise that might wake Sophie, who slept in a similar bedroom across from hers. She went down the hall, passing the room that her mother used as a study. The bathroom was big and old-fashioned, with an enormous tub that stood on claw feet. She brushed her teeth hurriedly, anxious to get dressed and outside.

As the stairs creaked under her feet, Beth thought with pleasure that old houses had many voices. Standing by the sink in the large farmhouse kitchen, she drank a glass of orange juice. Out the window a red-winged blackbird swooped to the ground, picked something up, and flew back to his nest in one of the apple trees. Maybe he has babies, Beth thought. She smiled as she headed out to feed the horses.

Behind the kitchen was a screened-in porch. A passageway led from the porch to the barn. Beth slid back the barn door and went in. Sun filtered through the high window, and dust motes floated in the shaft of light. Beth scooped grain out of a huge sack and put it in bins in each stall. She always brought the horses in to feed so that Charmin' would not eat his food and then go after Dolly's, too.

There was the rush of a barn swallow gliding up and over the hayloft. A field mouse scurried across the floor. The barn had a rich musty smell, and Beth felt a rush of joy. She was inexplicably and gloriously happy.

Bang, bang, bang: Charmin' had heard her and was signaling to her at the back door. She laughed out loud.

Taking his halter, she led him inside, and Dolly, puppylike, followed and went obediently into her own stall. While they ate, Beth filled their water buckets. Would she someday live on a farm like this, she wondered. Here she had such a sense of having come home.

After the chores were finished, Beth turned the horses out again and decided to take a walk. She went down the lane to the small enclosed pasture and then through an open gate into the larger one. Beth remembered her mother saying it covered some twenty acres. She walked until she came to a pretty brook where the water meandered over a rocky bed. It flowed and Beth followed its course along, finally stopping when she found a stand of pines. It was very still, almost cathedral-like, in among the tall, deep green trees. There was no brush or undergrowth, just a rust-colored cushion of needles squishing under her feet. Once through the evergreens, Beth came to the split-rail fence that bordered the property on the east. She climbed it and followed the old logging road, overgrown with lack of use. It brought her back to Pumpkin Hill Road about a half mile below the farm.

A dog barked, and she looked up to see a black labrador guarding the driveway of a green-shuttered farmhouse just below her. "It's all right, feller," she called to him. He took a few steps toward her. "Good boy," she said. Cautiously he came closer, his bark diminished in ferocity. Beth stopped and slowly extended her hand. "Come here, boy," she said. He walked over and sniffed her hand, tail barely wagging. "Good dog." Beth scratched him behind the ears.

"I guess I've got a friend." She laughed as the dog started following her up the road.

"Wheet. Wheet. Wheet." Beth heard a whistle and turned around. A gray-haired lady in a housedress and apron was standing on the farmhouse porch. "Come on, Freddy," she called to the lab, who stopped and looked at her, then at Beth.

"Hi." Beth waved.

"Mornin'," the woman answered. "Freddy bothering you?"

"No." She patted him. "I love dogs."

"Well, he likes kids. Misses my girl, who's away at school. You visiting around here?"

"I'm staying at Pretty Penny Farm," Beth answered.

"Are John and Alice up?" she asked, referring to the Helgesons.

"No. We've rented the farm for the summer."

"I just fried up a batch of doughnuts. Like to come in and have some?"

"Sure!" New Englanders certainly did not deserve their reputation for being cold and unfriendly, Beth thought.

They sat at a round oak table in a sunny kitchen, and the woman, whose named turned out to be Sarah Wentworth, plied Beth with doughnuts. The walk had given her an appetite, and she would have been embarrassed at eating three of the warm, crusty goodies except that Mrs. Wentworth insisted. "Have another one," she kept saying. "You're a growing girl."

Mrs. Wentworth was a widow with two grown sons who had married and moved away. Her only daughter was a sophomore at the state university. "She's going to be a vet. Come back here to practice," Sarah told Beth proudly. "Only one of the kids who's got the farm in her blood."

Beth thought of Dave. It sounded as if he wouldn't be coming back once he finished college. The thought made her sad, although she couldn't have explained why.

"Johnny, the oldest, does something with computers. He's living out in that place they call Silicon Valley," Mrs. Wentworth said. "I still think of valleys as places where rivers run and plants grow. I guess, nowadays, they raise word processors there 'stead of livestock." She laughed.

"I started learning about computers in junior high," Beth said. "Now they have them in grammar school. They're the big things now. Is your other son in business, too?"

"Just the opposite." Sarah Wentworth shook her head. "He's playing with some little band down New York way. I think Dawn—his wife—is doing most of the wage-earning. Billy's a songwriter by desire; a piano player by necessity."

"That's hard. They're both far away," Beth said. "Do you do the farming all by yourself?"

"Don't do much of it anymore. We used to keep dairy cattle and pigs and chickens, but I've given most of it up. I have a few hens and some beehives and about a quarter of an acre in garden. Keeps me busy."

"My mother's growing a vegetable garden, too," Beth told her.

"I've got some extra tomato seedlings if she's interested. You mention them to her."

"Thanks. I probably ought to get back." Beth pushed back her chair. "I left before anyone else was up."

"Just a minute." Mrs. Wentworth went over to a cabinet near the door. She came back with a brown bag and put half a dozen doughnuts in it.

"These are for your folks," she said.

"That is so nice." Beth took them gratefully.

"Now, you come back and see me and bring your mother," Sarah said.

"I'd love to," Beth promised.

When she got home, her parents and Sophie were sitting down to breakfast. Her father had cooked sausages and eggs and pancakes. All of their plates were full, but she was bothered by the sight of Sophie's plate heaped high with food.

Why did it disgust her when Sophie ate, she wondered. She liked seeing her father pour on the maple syrup and soak his pancakes in it. Her mother had as much to eat as Sophie, but that was all right. Her mother was thin. Beth had just stuffed herself on doughnuts, but she never gained an ounce. It was just that Sophie ought to do something about herself—she wouldn't be bad-looking if she were the right size. Her mother referred to her as "chunky." Beth thought she was more than that—thirty pounds overweight at least. Thirty pounds was the equivalent of a small child or six bags of sugar.

"I think I'll take Charmin' for a ride while it's still

nice and cool," she said, after giving them the doughnuts and telling them about Sarah Wentworth.

"Maybe Sophie'd like to go with you?" her father
suggested.

Sophie shook her head. "I don't know how to ride
yet," she said.

"Well, for heaven's sake, Beth," her father said,
"you ought to be able to teach her. You've had enough
lessons, Lord knows."

Beth sighed. "Do you want a lesson, Sophie?"

Sophie looked for a minute as if she was going to get
up. Beth was relieved when she settled back into her
chair. "I don't want to be a bother," she said.

"You're certainly not a bother," Charles Bridgewater
assured her. "I'm sure Beth would be glad to share
what she has learned. Wouldn't you, Beth?"

"I don't mind." Beth could not force herself to sound
enthusiastic.

"Not today," Sophie said quickly. "I'll spend time
getting to know Dolly better. Then you can give me a
lesson."

"I'll be back before lunch." Beth went out the door
before her father could try more persuasion.

She was currying Charmin' when her father came
into the barn. "What do you think of your summer so
far?" he asked.

"I love it." Beth picked up a brush and removed
some dirt from Charmin's foreleg.

"I guess there's no question of your not staying,
then?"

"I'd be happy staying here forever," Beth told him.

"How is it working out with Sophie?" he asked.

"All right. She goes her way, and I go mine." Beth put on the saddle pad.

"Is she having as good a time going her way as you are going yours?" her father asked.

"She seemed to be having a great time at the dance, didn't she?" Beth adjusted the saddle, then pulled hard on the cinch.

"Yes," he admitted. "But your mother tells me she has spent most of her time reading in her room or helping in the garden. Doesn't sound like much fun."

Beth slipped off the halter with one hand while working on the bridle with the other. She said nothing.

"I think she's a painfully shy girl, and you could help her." Charles walked next to Beth as she led Charmin' out of the barn. "She's a sweet person. It wouldn't hurt you to be friendly with her."

"Mom invited her, so don't try to make me feel guilty, okay?" Beth swung up into the saddle.

"Think it over, will you? It may be as important to you as it is to her," her father said quietly. "I have a feeling you're going to come through. This is the summer you're going to find out what stuff you're made of."

Her father had a real genius for laying it on her at times, Beth thought, making her look at herself in ways she wasn't sure she wanted to. She clucked to Charmin' and walked him down the driveway, then skirted the lawn in front of the house. Her father might be

right about the summer—not about her relationship
with Sophie, but about the summer. She had only been
on the farm a week, and already Riverdale looked different to her. And there was Dave Fuller. She got a
fluttery feeling in her stomach thinking about him. She
had only gone out with a boy once, and although she
talked a good game around her friends, really hadn't
wanted to date. That one time had been the worst, but
last night she had liked Dave's arm around her waist,
and the way he had looked at her.

She was in the meadow now on the far side of the
house. Charmin' tossed his head, putting pressure on
the bit. He did a little sideways dance as she kept him
in check. "Wanta run, don't you, boy?" His energy
seemed to flow into her knees as she tightened them
against him. "Go on, then." She tried to ease him into a
canter, but he quickly broke from it and they pounded
up the gentle incline. The horse took great bounding
leaps into the air. Exhilarated, she crouched lower in
the saddle, her heart thudding aginst his neck as he
gathered speed. With so much power under her, she
was on the edge of control. They flew across the
meadow. There was nothing for it but to take him out
on the dirt road. The hill got steeper. Surely he would
tire. But he seemed tireless, the dust flying beneath his
feet. They covered the half mile in what seemed like
seconds to Beth. Only as they approached the top
could she feel him respond to the pressure on the reins.
Her arms ached from the strain of pulling him back.
There was an open field on her right, and she angled

him into it, taking him again into a wide circle, stopping him on the second time around. She was sweating, her hands were wet, and she could feel her knees tremble as she let them relax. She found herself panting as if she had run up the hill herself. Quickly she dismounted and began to walk Charmin' around to cool down.

She looked about, wiping her forehead on her sleeve. This was what her father would call a vista. There were mountains to be seen in the distance on all sides. They rose, dark and commanding, in the soft summer morning.

She watched a pickup truck rattle up the dirt road. It pulled over and stopped. Clammy Ellis got out. "Mawning," he called. Beth grinned at the New Hampshire speech that took out r's in the middle of some words and added them to the ends of others.

"Hi, Clammy." She walked Charmin' over to meet him.

"I hadn't seen that colt run before," he said. "He sure hightailed it up that hill."

"Isn't he something?" She smiled, pleased at the compliment to Charmin'.

"It's getting where Josie's Babe needs some egging on." He patted Charmin's neck. The horse backed up and looked at Clammy warily. "I think this hoss might do it. How 'bout bringing him to the fairgrounds tomorrow so the Babe can get the feel of competition?"

"Wow!" Beth loved the idea. "That sounds like fun. How do I get there?"

"Percy's got a two-hoss rig. I'll pick you up. Can't ride 'em four miles, then expect 'em to race. We run early, though; eight o'clock—'fore the heat. Okay?"

"Great! I'll be ready," Beth agreed.

"See you then." Clammy waved and turned back to his truck.

On the ride back she thought about Dave. He had told her to keep Charmin' around the farm, but what harm could it do to take him to the fairground? Clammy would be there if Dave was worried about her getting hurt. There would be no reason for him to object.

"Your mother and Sophie are packing a picnic," her father told her as she came into the kitchen. "I've heard of a nice lake about ten miles from here."

"Sounds good. I could use a swim." Beth answered.

Sophie was finishing stuffing deviled eggs at the counter. "I'm not going to swim," she said. "I didn't bring a suit."

"You have an extra, don't you, Beth?" Elinor asked.

Beth pointed silently at Sophie's broad back and then at herself and shrugged.

Elinor grimaced, acknowledging her mistake, and said quickly, "Actually I have a nice black one-piece stretch suit that would look lovely with your blond hair, Sophie. I'll get it."

"Please don't bother, Mrs. Bridgewater. I don't care that much about swimming," Sophie said.

"Nonsense. You'll want to cool off." The master bedroom was off the living room, an arrangement common in many New England farmhouses, and Elinor ran in to get the suit.

"Get a move on, girls," Charles urged.

Beth was quick to change into her yellow bikini. Her tan from home had started to fade and was now uneven. Her face, arms, and neck were much darker from riding in the sun. She could use some sunbathing. As she came out into the upstairs hall, she heard a noise from Sophie's room and stopped. It sounded as if she were crying.

"Sophie?" She knocked on the door.

There was no answer, but the muffled sounds stopped.

"Sophie?" she said again.

The door opened a crack. "I'll b-b-be down soon."

"What's the matter?" Beth pushed on the door, and it opened enough for her to see Sophie standing in the black bathing suit, tears streaming down her face.

Sophie turned away and sat on the bed, shoulders hunched. "I can't go," she said defiantly. She began to cry again. "I can't—I won't—" She couldn't get the words out.

Beth looked down at her. White skin bulged around the straps, and Sophie's thighs ballooned against the black suit.

"Don't cry." Beth searched desperately for something to say. "Black makes people look thinner. Did you know that?" It wasn't exactly a lie. "I'll get you a tissue." There was a box on the dresser, and she put it down next to Sophie.

"I . . ." Sophie's shoulders were shaking. "I really can't go." She sniffled and reached for a tissue. "Tell your parents—I can't." Her face was contorted and red with crying.

"Ready, girls?" Charles called up the stairs.

Beth went to the door. "We'll be down soon, okay?" she called.

"Hurry it up," came the answer.

Beth ran into her room. She had an old sweatshirt of her father's that she liked to loaf around in. She was sure it would fit Sophie.

"Look, Sophie," she said. "Put this on. If you feel self-conscious in the suit, this will cover it up. Okay?"

Sophie twisted around to look at her.

"Come on." Beth put a hand on her arm. Sophie looked surprised at the touch. Beth handed her another tissue, and she wiped her eyes.

"Put it on," Beth said, giving her the sweatshirt. Sophie was still swallowing hard, but she pulled the shirt over her head.

Beth went into the bathroom and came back with a wet washcloth. Sophie wiped her face. "Thank you," she said.

"You take your time. I'll go tell them you'll be ready in a little while."

Sophie gave Beth a grateful look, and it made her uncomfortable. Sure she'd felt sorry for her, but that didn't change anything. They were just not the same type, so she hoped Sophie wasn't getting any ideas.

Her parents were sympathetic when she told them

about Sophie's crying. However, she thought her mother was less than subtle in the car when she broached the subject of dieting. "You know," Elinor said, "I just couldn't get into my white shorts. I think this country air is making us all eat too much."

"You look fine," Charles said, not realizing her ploy.

"I think it would be a good idea if we all cut down a bit," she said, nudging him. "What do you think, Beth?"

"I'm getting plenty of exercise," Beth answered. She refused to go along when her mother was being so obvious.

Sophie unexpectedly spoke up. "I'll go on a diet with you, Mrs. Bridgewater. I know I eat too much."

"Fine, Sophie. Eating too much is just a bad habit—a trap we all fall into very easily."

"I guess I've never been out of it," Sophie said. "Ever since I can remember, my father has cooked so many good things. He always wanted me to be healthy. 'We'll put meat on those bones,' he used to say to me when I was little. I guess we put too much meat on them."

Sophie had not been one to talk much, and they were all surprised by what was, for her, a long speech.

"At your age it won't take long to come off," Elinor assured her. "We'll start tomorrow, and you'll see."

"It will be easier dieting here than at home. I've tried sometimes, but my father gets hurt if I don't eat what he cooks. And I like to eat it, too."

"How old were you when your mother died?" Elinor

asked gently. Beth winced. Why did her mother have to pry like that?

Sophie did not seem to mind the question. "Five," she said.

"Ah, such a little girl." Elinor sighed. "And your father brought you up all by himself."

"When we lived in Buffalo, I had a lot of aunts and uncles. My mother's family. But then two years ago we moved to Riverdale. . . ." Her voice trailed off.

"Do you like Riverdale?" Charles asked.

"It's all right . . . maybe . . ." She hesitated. "No, I don't like it very much, really. It's pretty, a lot prettier than Buffalo. But in Buffalo we lived in a Polish neighborhood, and we were like everybody else. My father says it's better, though. He says it isn't good to be just with one sort of people."

But people in Riverdale were all alike, Beth thought. All the men commuted, and though some women did, too, most of them stayed at home until their kids went to college. Then they floated around taking courses or volunteering at the hospital. A few, like her mother, began careers of their own. And what about the kids? She thought about her group—they all dressed the same way and hung out in the same places. So Sophie had grown up in a Polish neighborhood; Beth had also grown up surrounded by her own kind. And had she ventured outside of her own turf any more than the people in Sophie's old world had? Worse than that, she admitted to herself. She and her friends never wanted to let anyone in. Let a Sophie come along, and they would ignore her or use her or pick on her. It made her uncomfortable to think about it.

Was this what her father had meant about the summer? Already she felt different from the Beth who had been editor of the ninth grade yearbook, vice-president of the junior high, best friend of the most popular girl in school. That Beth hadn't bothered herself with these stupid, prickly ideas. She hadn't had to. Beth looked over at Sophie wrapped up in the big sweatshirt. Motherless, overweight, probably lonely Sophie.

Why hadn't they left Sophie and her problems back in Riverdale?

CHAPTER

5

Beth had already saddled Charmin' and was waiting in the driveway the next morning when Clammy pulled up in a two-horse trailer. He opened the back door, which let down into a ramp. Then he came over and took Charmin's bridle from Beth. "I'll load him," he said. "Let's go, Charmin'."

The horse backed up, tugging against the strap. "Hey there, boy, let's not be hard to get along with," Clammy said, and clucked to the horse.

"Come on, Charmin'," Beth coaxed, pulling on the other side of the bridle and patting his neck. The chestnut moved forward, but balked when he got to the ramp. He dug his front hooves in and pulled his head back as far as he could. Both Clammy and Beth tugged, but he wouldn't budge. Every time they relaxed their grip, he backed up farther. "Let him go a minute," Beth said.

"Whatcha going to do with the old mule?" Clammy asked, stepping back.

"Watch who you're calling a mule." Beth fished a sugar cube from her shirt pocket and gave it to the horse. She whispered to him and rubbed her cheek against his nose, then gave him another.

"Danged if I'd give him sugar," Clammy said.

Beth took out another cube and extended her hand into the trailer. Charmin' moved forward, and Beth did, too. "See," she said once he was loaded, "he doesn't like to be bossed. He likes to make his own decisions."

The fairground was four miles away. It looked like a large town park. At one end was a grandstand. "Different bands will play there every night during the fair," Clammy said. "Holds about five hundred people." There was a large mowed area. "Rides and hot dog stands go there." Clammy pointed. Next were several sheds. "All kinds of livestock contests," he reminisced. "I 'member when it was the best part of belongin' to 4H—bringing our calves and chickens and pigs to the fair. Sure loved winnin' those ribbons. I slept in that shed one night. I laugh about it now, but I was worried about Ima and Ura."

"Who?" Beth asked.

"Ima Pig and Ura Hog. They were some pair. They won in their division."

Beth laughed. "I love the names," she said.

"Now, that"—Clammy jerked his head toward a pretty colonial building—"is where they have the women's stuff. You know, the cakes and the pies, and the needle whatevers. Also have some contests there—watermelon eating, that kind of thing."

"The fair sounds like fun," Beth said.

"Pretty much, I'll tell you," Clammy agreed. "And here's where the best of it will be." He pulled into a paddock area and parked. There were low, long stables and an oval track with a pretty white rail fence. In the middle were green grass and beds of geraniums and marigolds.

Charmin' was eager to get out of the trailer and skittered backward down the ramp. Josie's Babe made no such clatter but backed smoothly and even elegantly from the small van. Beth hadn't seen her clearly before. "What a beautiful horse, and what a lady!" she said. The mare was a silver gray with a black mane and tail. Her glossy coat shone in the sun. She tossed her head as if she understood what Beth had said.

"We'll warm 'em up before we run 'em," Clammy said. "Track's a half mile. We'll do two slow go-rounds; then we'll race."

Beth tried to keep Charmin' to a walk to limber up slowly from the trailer ride, but he was hard to hold back. She pulled on the reins, and his back feet danced first to one side of the track and then the other, moving forward in half circles. Josie's Babe maintained a high-stepping, even, fast walk. Finally Clammy moved the gray into a trot, and Charmin' pushed ahead eagerly.

He wanted to go! Her arms were aching by the time they completed the first round, and Clammy started to canter. She relaxed the pressure, and Charmin' sprinted ahead in an all-out gallop.

"Hey, we're not racin' this time," Clammy called.

"Tell Charmin' that," Beth yelled over her shoulder, pulling back on the reins. The horse showed no interest in slowing down, and they were back at the starting line before she could get him stopped.

"Easy, boy." She patted his neck and turned him to face Clammy and Josie's Babe, who came up at a smooth canter.

"If you're so all-fired eager to run, Charmin', we'll show you how it's done," Clammy said, grinning. "Line up with me, Beth, and we'll go on the count of three."

Charmin' snorted and danced around. Josie's Babe stood head up, eyes forward. When they were roughly together, Clammy counted. "One. Two. Three!"

Beth wasn't used to going directly into a canter. This was something horse show training had not prepared her for. She had trouble getting the right lead, and Josie's Babe was well down the track. Charmin' was all over the place, drifting close to the outside rail. There seemed to be no communion between horse and rider. Beth could have kicked herself. It was the bad start that had caused the problem. Josie's Babe beat them easily.

"You'd be better off if you shortened your stirrups," Clammy advised her as they were getting ready for the second run. "Look at mine."

Of course, she should have known. She'd seen enough pictures of jockeys and watched the Derby with her dad every year on TV. Jockeys sat like Clammy, their legs like closed V's. She got off, and Clammy helped her adjust the stirrups. He had to give her a hand up. It felt weird. She was scrunched up and couldn't get her heels down. It was a long way to the ground, and for the first time in years she was afraid she might fall off.

It made her nervous. She wasn't sure she could sit a canter, let alone Charmin's pounding, leaping gallop.

"One. Two. Three!" Beth fell forward on Charmin's neck, anticipating his lunge. He stumbled, and she grabbed his mane. Once more, Josie's Babe had moved smoothly into the front and was galloping away from them, little clouds of her dust stirring the air. Charmin' was cantering, but it was a ragged gait, and Beth knew it was her fault. If you weren't in control, a horse could sense it right away. It made her mad to do so badly something she liked.

"Takes a while to get the hang of the stirrups," Clammy said when they came up, long after Josie's Babe had finished the run. The gray looked as if she were eyeing them curiously. Well, she was a racehorse. Charmin' wasn't, and Beth was surely no jockey.

They dismounted and walked the horses around to cool them down. Charmin' was sweating. Josie's Babe didn't even look warm.

"Better not run Charmin' more'n another time or two today," Clammy said. "Have to work him up to it."

"He's all right," Beth muttered. "I'm the one who's having trouble."

"Get your weight up, off his back, next time," Clammy advised. "He'll run better. Leave some air between you and the saddle."

"How'd you learn so much about riding?" Beth asked. "If there's only racing at the fair once a year, you can't have seen much."

"Read up on it," he answered. "And I go hang around down at Rockingham any chance I get."

"What's Rockingham?"

"Only real racetrack in the state. They get some good hosses there. I shovel out the stables and hang around the bugs—"

"Bugs? You mean horseflies?"

Clammy started laughing, head thrown back and eyes closed. "Hossflies?" He laughed again.

"What's so funny?"

"Bugs are apprentice jockeys." He got himself under control. "They call them that because they have little marks—bugs—next to their names in the program."

"Well, aren't you a bug, then?" Beth asked.

"Nope. Have to be licensed. And to get licensed, you have to hook up with a trainer and work in the barns first. When I'm done with school, I aim to do just that. For now, this is the best I can do. Sure like to win this race," he said. "It'd help to get someone interested in taking me on."

A Jeep pulled into the driveway by the paddock area, and Percy Fuller and Dave got out. Dave was frowning when he walked up to them. "What are you doing here?" he asked Beth.

Beth blushed. She probably should have gotten his permission. "I'm sorry," she said. "Clammy asked me to come. Since I was with him, I thought it would be all right."

"I didn't want that horse off the farm," he answered.

"Guess it's my fault," Clammy apologized. "Josie's Babe was getting a little lazy. She's just been breezing in the workouts. I figured as how another hoss would pep her up, git her to run flat out. Didn't mean to cause a problem."

"No harm done." Percy Fuller put his hand on Dave's arm. "That hoss of yours needs to be worked, Dave. Not good for a high-strung colt like that to be lazing in the pasture. Hosses are like people. Work keeps 'em healthy."

"Beth's riding him at the farm. That works him out enough," Dave insisted.

"But if riding him here's gonna help us win that race, don't make much sense not to, does it?"

When Dave said nothing, his father turned to Clammy. "Let's see you take them around," he said, pulling out a stopwatch.

Beth was nervous as she remounted. It had been bad enough when there had been just her and Clammy. But now with Mr. Fuller and Dave looking on, it was worse—especially Dave, who did not look a bit happy.

"Now, Beth," Clammy said to her as they took their

places on the starting line, "once he moves, raise up in that saddle."

Percy Fuller leaned on the fence, holding a stopwatch in one hand. "Ready . . . set . . . and *go!*" Clammy broke ahead of her, but Beth's start was better than the last ones. She pushed down on her heels, raising her body, and leaned over the horse's neck. It still didn't feel natural, but she wasn't afraid anymore, and she could feel Charmin' moving smoothly under her. She looked ahead as Josie's Babe took a corner so close, it seemed as if she would brush the fence. Of course, Beth thought. That was important. The closer to the inside, the less distance to cover. They were coming into the backstretch now and she edged Charmin' closer to the inside as they galloped for the far turn. They shaved it, and Beth could have whooped with excitement. She urged Charmin' on into the homestretch. She felt the surge of his power. He was gaining on Josie's Babe! It was like being in a car going seventy, overtaking one going fifty. The sensation was exhilarating, but there was a large gap to close. She saw Clammy using the crop. Josie's Babe crossed the line two lengths ahead. Charmin' shot past her right after. At least this time Josie's Babe was sweating!

When they jogged back to Percy Fuller, he was smiling. "Not bad," he said to Clammy. "You were twenty-five seconds at the quarter and fifty seconds at the half, and you finished at a minute three. Mite slow on the finish, but the other times were good."

"She was driving most of the way," Clammy said, "but I felt her starting to quit near the end. Had to use the whip."

"Well, you have to," Percy said. "Don't let her quit." He turned to Beth. "You did awful good for a novice. Thought we were goin' to have a photo finish."

"I could have done better." Beth was glowing with the elation of the homestretch ride. "I could really feel him move. If I'd started sooner . . ."

"This isn't a racehorse we're talking about," Dave interrupted her, "so you're not going to get him to run like one. I see no point in working him out down here."

"Sure is if he helps the Babe get her speed up," Percy said. " 'Sides, Dave, look at that hoss. Look at those bones and that straight nose and those wide-spaced eyes. Those eyes are smart as anything. He's a Thoroughbred."

"He wasn't good enough for the Eatons, and they know horses. They're into big-time racing. They never even entered him. He's a good hack horse. That's what Curtis told me when I won him."

Percy shrugged. "Nice-looking hoss," he said. He walked over and petted Josie's Babe. "We're counting on you, little girl, so don't you go loafing."

"She's going to be ready for that race," Clammy promised. "Wonder what hosses she's going to be up against."

"Season'll be about over down at Rockingham," Percy answered. "Might get a ringer or two from down theah looking for an easy purse, but we'll surprise them."

"We don't usually get too many, though. They think this is the boonies," Clammy said.

"Some. We'll get some." Percy stuck the watch back in his pocket. "Got about five entries from the county here, but none I'm worried 'bout. I know 'em all, and the Babe can take them."

"Why won't there be more outsiders?" Beth asked.

" 'Cause this here's what horsemen call limbo," Percy told her. "Racing at the fair's mostly a local event and mostly for fun. The horse racing association doesn't have anything to do with it, so you don't have to have licensed jockeys or trainers or handicaps or any of that. But there's this one race a local fella set up way back that has a big purse. He was kind of an eccentric, you might say. Hear tell he was some relation of a famous family who wanted the quiet life. Anyway, he had this bee in his bonnet about getting Thoroughbred horse raising started 'round heah. Didn't have much luck with his own hosses, but left some kind of endowment in his will to encourage folks around here to try."

"And there are a lot of farmers around here who now dream of winning the Kentucky Derby." Dave's tone was sarcastic.

"Nothing wrong with dreams, Dave," Percy said. "People get tired of just keeping their nose to the grindstone. Speaking of which, we better be gettin' back to camp. There's a trail ride this morning."

"When would you like me to come and work?" Beth asked. She had not forgotten that she was getting the use of Charmin' in exchange for helping at the camp.

"Seems to me any day you work out with Clammy heah, you're doin' your part," Percy answered. "Your friend arrived just before we left, and she's helping Mrs. Fuller with the breakfast dishes. Say, has she ridden little Dolly yet?"

Beth shook her head. "She's afraid."

"But she showed up to help anyway. Mighty nice young'un." Percy waved. "See you later."

" 'Bye." Dave turned and followed his father.

"You ready for another go-round?" Clammy asked.

Beth nodded. If she could do it right this time, she'd show Dave that Charmin' could run. Of course, he wouldn't be there to see it, but she would prove it anyway.

This time it was Josie's Babe who got off to a slow start. Beth was elated to be leading for once. The chestnut moved smoothly down the field. She looked over her shoulder to see where the gray was. She had a good edge on her even before she rounded the home-stretch turn.

"Come on, boy," she whispered, leaning down close to his neck and urging him on. Nothing happened. There was not that feeling of exhilaration, of speed, that she'd had on the last run. She looked back again. Clammy and Josie's Babe did not seem to be gaining. The finish line was just ahead. "Move it, Charmin'," she urged, irritated by a sense of frustration she did not understand.

They were across. They'd beaten the gray. Why wasn't she more excited, she wondered as she pulled Charmin' up.

"You rode better that time," Clammy complimented her as they unsaddled the horses.

"Something didn't feel right," she answered. "But we won anyway."

"What didn't feel right was the pace." Clammy walked his mount around to cool her down. "Neither one was driving. The Babe saw you were ahead and didn't even bother to run."

"I had the feeling Charmin' wasn't trying either."

"That's what you call 'breezing,'" he explained. "Hosses are funny critters. Guess he figured there was no sense in running all by himself."

"I don't get it," Beth said.

"You get a hoss in a race. If he looks around and sees he's outclassed, he's not going to run nearly as good as he did in his workouts. If he sees the rest are losers, he's going to take first place but prob'ly not try too hard. Now, if he sees he's got competition but has a chance, he'll prob'ly run his best race."

"Then how can you be so sure Josie's Babe can beat horses from Rockingham? Aren't they liable to be better?" Beth asked.

"Nothing's ever sure in a horse race." Clammy grinned. "But I'm betting she's got class, and if we're tuned up, both of us, we can do it."

"What will happen if you do win?" Beth took the cloth Clammy offered and started to rub Charmin' down.

"I think Percy's planning to put her on the county fair circuit. If she makes it there, then he'd have to consider running her at some of the smaller tracks."

As they were talking, a red pickup pulled into the paddock area. Two men got out of the car. One was a short, stocky man with a mustache, dressed in a business suit. The other was medium-height. He was dressed in khakis and wore cowboy boots. His face was tanned, and although he did not look to be middle-aged yet, there were lines around his eyes and mouth.

"Good morning," the older man said. "This the Warrington County fairgrounds?"

"Mornin'," Clammy answered. "You got it."

"You working out those horses for the fair?" the other man asked.

"Ayeh," Clammy replied. "Just finished up a workout."

"Must be a pretty big time for you folks, huh?" The taller man smiled. "Campaigning your horses at the fair."

Clammy did not smile back. "You lookin' for somebody round heah?" he asked.

"Just looking over the track." The stocky man gestured. "Go see what you think of it, Al," he said to the other man.

"Right, Mr. Carl." He pushed through the gate.

"Nice-looking horse you've got there, little lady,"

Mr. Carl said to Beth. "Are you riding him in some of these contests?"

Beth shook her head.

"How about you, son? You and your filly running?"

"Ayeh." Clammy started leading Josie's Babe to the trailer. "We're going for the Pearson Prize."

"Ahhh. That's the big one. We're probably going to see you there if my trainer likes the track." He walked over to the fence. "What do you think, Al?"

"Looks all right," Al answered. "Needs a little work, but the base is good."

"You been racing at Rockingham?" Clammy had stopped when he heard they were interested in bringing a horse to the fair.

"Uh-huh," Mr. Carl answered.

"How you done this season?" Clammy asked.

"Fair." He looked at Charmin' intently as Beth walked him toward the trailer. "That is certainly one good-looking piece of horseflesh," he said.

"What kind of horse you bringing up?" Clammy asked.

"A winner." The man laughed.

"Be 'bout ten of those in the race, I 'magine, if you believe everything you hear beforehand," Clammy retorted. "Let's load 'em together, Beth," he said. "You'll probably have less trouble with Charmin'."

He was right: the horses loaded with no fuss. As they got into the truck, the man named Al called, "See you at the races, kid."

"Well," Clammy said as he leaned on the ignition,

"plain to see they think we're hicks. We'll just have to show 'em."

Beth wished with all her heart she were going to be in the race. She and Charmin' could show them, too.

CHAPTER 6

It was a beautiful summer morning in mid-July. There was a little time before Clammy would come to pick her up, so Beth walked down to her favorite apple tree near the little pond. Long, skinny darning needles darted over the surface of the water. The smell of clover was sweet. She grabbed a limb and swung herself up easily, loving the healthy strength of her body. It had been a summer out of a book.

A screen door slammed at the farm, and she looked up to see Sophie turning on the sprinklers to water the flower beds that bordered the house. Even Sophie had turned out to be not half bad. Beth didn't have to compete with her the way she did with Amy and the kids back home. Sophie liked to hear all the details of the workouts with Clammy. The first day she had come home and told her about beating Josie's Babe, Sophie had been almost as excited as she was. It was nice to have someone to talk to who wasn't just waiting for you to finish so she could begin talking. Sophie was okay. Not that Beth would be friends with her at home. The thought made her uncomfortable, and she put it out of her mind.

She climbed up to her favorite branch and settled herself in the V with her back against the trunk. She liked to come here to be alone and think about Dave, to go over every little detail of their meetings. She liked almost as much to think about him as to be with him. They hadn't had a date or anything, but he stopped by the farm a lot when he was out running. She always made sure she was around in the late afternoon when the heat of the day was fading.

Yesterday had been, as they said in New Hampshire, a scorcher. At six o'clock she'd fed the horses and turned them into the lane. She hadn't heard him come up behind her, and she jumped when she felt his hand on her shoulder. "Buy me a drink of cold water?" he asked.

He'd been wearing a T-shirt and gym shorts. His hair was wet and curled close to his head. You weren't supposed to admire boys' legs, she thought, but his were smooth and tanned, not skinny or fat, just sort of compact and strong-looking.

They had gone back to the house, and she'd brought a pitcher of iced tea out to the porch. The old-fashioned ceiling fan stirred up the air and made it seem cooler.

She had started telling him about Charmin'. Now that she was comfortable with the jockey seat, they beat Josie's Babe about half the time.

"I'm up to here with horses." He put his hand to his chin. "I hear about them from my father and from Clammy. Give me a break, will you?"

Her feelings had been hurt, and her face must have showed it, because he leaned over and squeezed her arm. "Sorry," he said. "I didn't mean to snap at you." He looked distracted, though his words were kind.

"Is something wrong?" she asked.

"I got a letter from school today. They're putting me on probation for next semester." He stared down at his feet.

"That's terrible," Beth exclaimed. "How could they do that to you?" She was sure they were to blame and not Dave.

"Easy. I flunked a couple of courses." His face looked serious now, worried. "My mother'll have a coronary if she finds out about it."

"Well, don't tell," Beth said. "Just go back and make them up, and everything will be okay."

"Not that simple." He rattled the ice in his tea. "Unless the coach can talk the powers-that-be out of it, probation will mean I'm off the track team and lose my scholarship."

"Oh, no!"

"Yeah. And if that happens, I'm out of school. I can't get the tuition."

"What about your folks?" she asked.

"Uh-uh. No way. Even if he had it, which he doesn't, my father would never bail me out after I'd messed up like this. He's a great believer in 'folks takin' the consequences of their acshuns.'" Dave imitated his father's accent.

"Well"—Beth tried to think of a way out—"if you get off probation after the first semester, would you get your scholarship back?"

"I might. But I can't get off probation if I'm not in school."

"Couldn't you borrow the money for the first semester?" Beth suggested.

"Where? Curtis Eaton, my roommate, is loaded, and he'd lend me the money, but he had his allowance cut off, and he's not old enough to tap his trust funds."

"That's a shame. How'd he lose his allowance?" she asked.

"An argument with his family. I'm really not free to talk about it, see?"

Beth got red. "I didn't mean to be nosy," she said, embarrassed.

"It's okay. You weren't. I didn't mean to snap. It wasn't you. It's just . . . uh . . . forget it." He leaned over and pulled her braid. "You're a good kid."

She had put her hair in a thick braid because of the heat. Now she was sorry. It must make her look about twelve years old.

Thinking about it now, she wondered again for about the tenth time if he thought of her as a kind of little sister. She pulled a leaf off the apple tree and threw it to the ground. No, she reassured herself. He had confided in her, hadn't he? As he left, he had said, "Listen. This is just between the two of us, okay? I don't want anyone else to know about it."

She wished there were some way she could help him. Taking hold of a branch in front of her with both hands, she swung out and back and forth, and dropped to the ground. Then she walked up toward the barn, stopping to pick a daisy.

"He loves me. He loves me not," she said to herself silently as she plucked the petals.

"Beth!" Her mother's voice calling from the garden startled her. She quickly threw the flower to the ground. "Come here, please."

Her mother was staking tomato plants. "Look," she said. "They've got blossoms. We'll be eating tomatoes before you know it."

"That's nice," Beth answered. "The garden's looking good."

"Yes, isn't it." Elinor straightened up. "Do you think you could give me a hand with it this morning? There are a million things to do. The lettuce needs transplanting. The weeds are starting to take over—"

"I'm waiting for Clammy," Beth interrupted. "We have to go to the track and work out."

"I'm getting a little sick of this, Beth." Her mother's tone was sharp. "You're always fooling around with that horse. I would think you'd make a little time to help when you're needed."

"That's my job." Beth was defensive. "Remember? I

have to help the Fullers in exchange for Charmin'."

"And when you're not helping the Fullers, as you call it, you're washing the horse or cleaning his toes. And when you're not doing that, you're off mooning around or walking in the woods."

"Mooning around" stung. Beth was furious. "What's wrong with you, anyway? You're the one who dragged me up here. Now that I like it and I'm happy, you're going to spoil it."

"I can't see how asking for a little help is spoiling anything." Elinor turned back to her plants.

"It isn't that. It's your nasty attitude. You make everything I'm doing sound so dumb." Beth hated it when her mother started an argument and then turned away. "And you don't clean a horse's toes, you clean his hooves!"

"Hooves. Toes. I could care less," her mother said.

"That's obvious."

"Beth." Elinor sighed. "Let's not argue."

"You started it." Beth glared.

"Well, you do seem awfully wrapped up in yourself. You don't have time to help me. You ignore Sophie—"

"I do not! I talk to her!"

"If a monologue at the dinner table about Charmin's performance at the fairgrounds can be considered talking to someone, then you talk, I guess. But the poor kid tries so hard. She's gone on a diet. She helps me in the kitchen. She helps me in the garden. I'd just like to see you really pay a little attention to her, see that she has some fun."

How could her mother accuse her of monologues at the dinner table? She was excited about the horse. Who wouldn't be? It wasn't her fault that Sophie was afraid of horses. And it wasn't her fault she was here. "Well, I'll tell you something," she said, striking back, "you can make me live with Sophie Chmielewski, but you can't make me like her!"

"Beth Bridgewater!" Her mother whirled on her, then stopped, looking stricken. "Oh, no!"

Beth turned in time to see Sophie disappear around the corner of the barn. She covered her face with her hands.

"Look what you've done!" Elinor gasped.

"I'll find her." Beth didn't know how she'd face Sophie, but she knew she had to. She began to run. Once behind the barn, she spotted Sophie running up the hill in the meadow. "Sophie," she called. "Wait! Please."

Sophie did not turn around. Beth raced after her. As she came up to her, Sophie threw herself on the ground, sobbing.

"I'm sorry." Beth dropped down next to her. "I feel terrible. I didn't mean it, Sophie. Honest I didn't."

The weeping girl turned her face away.

"I was mad at my mother, that's all. It didn't have anything to do with you." Even to Beth that sounded like a feeble excuse. What could she say to undo those spiteful words?

"I want to go home," Sophie wailed.

"Please don't say that. That would be awful." Beth couldn't stand the thought. What would her family think of her if she were the cause of Sophie's leaving? What would she think of herself? "Sophie, listen, please. I didn't mean it. I do want to be your friend. Why wouldn't I? You're a really kind, good person. Look at all the ways you help my mother. And Mr. Fuller just raves about the way you've helped at his camp. Everybody likes you." As Beth said it, she realized it was true. Sophie never complained, and she was always doing things for others. "My mother's right. I have been selfish. It's just that Charmin' is like a dream come true. I guess I've been so wrapped up in him, I haven't thought of anyone else."

Sophie rubbed her eyes and swallowed, trying to stop the tears. "I don't care about that—" Her voice broke. "I don't want to be in the way here. . . ." Her body shook.

"You're not in the way. You've got to believe me. I didn't mean what I said. My mother was on my back, and I wanted to spite her. Look, Sophie, the fair's in a couple of weeks. After that I'll have more time to do stuff. I'll bet I can even teach you to ride. Wouldn't that be fun?"

Sophie shook her head. "I'm too . . . fat. And I'm . . . clumsy."

"No you're not," Beth assured her. She pulled on the waistband of Sophie's jeans. "See. These jeans are big on you already. And how can you say you're clumsy? The way you dance? You're really graceful."

"But when I get nervous, I feel like there's too much

of me. I bump into things. Look how I fell off that horse."

"You'll get over that. Why, you've already gotten so you'll go up and pet Dolly in the pasture. You'll see, Sophie. I'll make a rider out of you before this summer's over. I promise."

"You don't have to be nice to me because of what you said. I know I'm not like Amy and your real friends. I know they make fun of me." Sophie was swallowing her words, and Beth could barely hear them.

"You know what makes you different from them?" Beth faced the unpleasant truth. "You're kinder than they are. It's not that I don't like them or don't want to be in with them, because I do, but they can be mean. You wouldn't know how to be mean, and that makes you a better person."

"You're just trying to make me feel better." Sophie's breath came in little gasps. "You never wanted to do anything with me before. Now you say you do because you feel guilty."

There was truth in what Sophie said. But it wasn't the whole truth. She wanted to make up for the pain she had caused Sophie. And she wanted to be able to live with herself. Her meanness made her like the friends she had just criticized. It was odd that she wanted to be part of them, but she didn't want to be like them.

None of them would ever make friends with Sophie.

None of them would dare. They would be afraid her unpopularity would infect them—like a communicable disease.

"I'm going to be different, Sophie. That's a promise."

"Don't be nice to me because you're sorry for me. That would only make things worse." Sophie looked directly at Beth. She wasn't crying anymore, and there was a defiant edge in her voice that Beth admired.

"Right." Beth nodded. "I understand."

Her mother, looking worried, was coming up the hill. "Clammy's here," she called.

"Why don't you come watch the workout today?" Beth got to her feet. "I'd like you to see Charmin' run. Honest. After all I've told you, you should see for yourself."

"I don't think so." Sophie looked away. "I'm kind of a mess right now."

"Go wash up," Beth urged. "By the time I get Charmin' tacked up and in the trailer, you'll look fine."

"Sophie." Her mother came up to them and leaned down to squeeze Sophie's shoulder.

"I'm trying to talk her into coming to the fairground," Beth told her.

"Good idea!" Elinor was obviously trying to lighten the mood. "Go see if all those stories Beth tells are true. You'd think Charmin' was Man o' War to hear her tell it."

Sophie shook her head.

"Maybe you'd feel more like it later?" Elinor suggested. "I'm going downtown, and I could drop you off."

"I'll be looking for you." Beth started to hurry off, then turned. "I'll feel lousy if you don't show."

The workout was fantastic. It was as if the efforts of the last few weeks had come together for both Beth and Charmin'. The Fullers, her mother, and Sophie arrived almost at the same time. Beth knew as she waited at the starting line for the signal to go that she had something special to show them. She felt keyed up but sure of herself. The chestnut was alert and eager.

"Thirty seconds." Percy Fuller looked at the watch in his hand. "Twenty. Ten. Five. Go!"

Beth leaned forward, her hands holding the reins close to Charmin's neck. "Go, boy, go," she whispered. It was almost as if he switched gears. He seemed to move from a bounding, pounding pace to a leaping, flying one. Beth had never felt such exhilaration. This horse loved to run, and, confident now, she loved being part of the exploding energy. She had learned not to look back, to concentrate solely on her race. She could sense, however, that Josie's Babe wasn't even a threat. They rounded the turn for the homestretch, and she felt as if she were airborne. Charmin' summoned more power, and they flew past the finish line.

She was trembling with excitement and could hardly talk as she dismounted in front of the little group.

"Well, you beat her hollow." Mr. Fuller was looking

at the watch as if he couldn't believe it. "Didn't bother to time you, Clammy." He held up the instrument. "I stopped it when Beth went over the line. Fifty-eight seconds. That's a time would stand up anywheres."

"That was very exciting, honey." Elinor squeezed her arm. "I see why you get so worked up about it. Don't you, Sophie?"

Beth looked at Sophie.

"It was beautiful," Sophie agreed. "Charmin' looked like he was ten feet off the ground."

Beth smiled at her. "Thanks, Sophie."

" 'Pears to me you got a racehorse, son." Percy nudged his son. Dave hadn't said anything. He ought to be thrilled, Beth thought.

"A fluke," he said finally.

"It was not!" Beth was incensed that he wouldn't give the horse his due. "He's been getting faster every day, hasn't he, Clammy?"

"Ayeh." Clammy was unsmiling. He looked at Percy Fuller. "The Babe is a good filly," he said, "better'n most, but she's never clocked a time like that. Don't think she will, either."

It must have been hard for him to say that, Beth thought. She knew how he'd been counting on the gray. But Charmin' was better. He'd just proved it. She felt her heart thumping. They had to know which horse could win the race.

"Could be we're entering the wrong hoss," Mr. Fuller said, echoing her thoughts.

Beth held her breath. Could it really be going to

happen? Would she really get to ride in the fair?

"No," Dave said. "Josie's Babe is the right horse. You can't count on Charmin' repeating that performance, and at least Josie's Babe is consistent."

"You can't argue 'gainst that clock, Dave," his father answered. "You got to put in the hoss that *can* do it. It'll be up to Clammy to get him to do it."

Up to Clammy! Beth turned and stared at Mr. Fuller in dismay, then buried her head in Charmin's neck. She couldn't let them see her face.

No one noticed her. They were too involved with the argument. "Clammy's not used to the horse," Dave said. "He should ride one he knows."

"He's got two weeks to get used to him. If little Beth can get that kind of run out of him, then Clammy sure can," Percy said.

"What's the matter with Josie's Babe all of a sudden? You've been talking about nothing but that horse for a year now," Dave argued.

"She's good, but she's not any fifty-eight seconds good, and I'm not so stubborn I can't see it." Percy squinted at him. "What's your trouble? Seems like you oughta be tickled silly you've turned up with a winner."

"Racing's a dirty business, and I don't want any part of it," Dave answered. "It's my horse, and he isn't running!" His face was red and angry.

"You got some awful funny ideas in a year at college," Percy said. "Now, you know how we're depending on that money. . . . We'll talk about this later." He walked over and put his hand on Beth's shoulder. "What's the matter, child?" he asked.

Beth didn't look at him. "Nothing," she muttered, her face pressed against the horse's neck.

"You should be jumpin' up and down after what you just did," Mr. Fuller said, patting her, " 'stead of standing here wiltin'. The heat and the excitement gettin' to you?"

She nodded. She didn't trust herself to talk.

"Do you feel faint, dear?" Her mother spoke up anxiously.

Why didn't they just leave her alone? She felt trapped, afraid she'd cry if she talked; afraid they'd keep at her if she didn't. "No," she managed.

"There's a water fountain on the other side of the stable. Let's go get a drink of water." Dave touched her arm. "She's all right, Mrs. Bridgewater," he said.

"Look—you think Charmin's going to race and you want to ride him," Dave said once they were out of earshot. "Isn't that it?'

"I don't want to talk about it right now, okay?" She sounded angrier than she meant to, but it was either get mad or cry. She wasn't going to bawl like a baby in front of him.

"Okay, Beth, but there's something you have to understand. Even if Charmin' were going to race—which he isn't—there is no way you could ride. Those professional jockeys would make mincemeat out of you."

"Just because I'm a girl?" Her temper flared.

"Hang on, I didn't say that. You're inexperienced,

and you're naïve. That's what I meant." He looked serious—and upset. "And there are a lot of people, not owners necessarily, but people who make a living out of fixing horse races, who aren't very pleasant types. Here"—he pressed the button on the water fountain—"cool down."

Beth took a long drink. It eased the tightness in her throat. When she finished, she stood back and Dave leaned over the fountain.

"Hey, little girl, nice ride."

Beth looked across the street. A man was leaning out of a red pickup truck. He looked somehow familiar, but she couldn't place him.

"Thanks," she called.

He waved his hand, started the truck, and drove off.

"Who was that?" Dave asked.

Beth shrugged. "I don't know. Someone who saw the workout, I guess."

"Someone was watching?" Dave's tenseness surprised her.

"So what? People stop to watch sometimes. There were a whole bunch of kids the other day. It's nice. You feel like there's an audience, and you try harder, you know? Like it was the race. . . ." Her voice trailed off.

"Now, stop feeling bad, Beth," Dave said. "I intend to see that Charmin' does not run in that race. You and I will be in the bleachers cheering on Josie's Babe."

"He should run. Even if I can't ride him, he should run. I don't know why you're so against it. Listen"—

the thought suddenly struck her—"you might even get some of that money for college."

"Not that way." Dave looked grim.

"I don't understand you," Beth said.

"Join the group." He sounded bitter. "Neither does my father."

They both heard the sound at the same time and turned to the fence. Clammy was riding Charmin' down the track.

Dave put a hand on her shoulder. "It's all right to cry," he said.

CHAPTER 7

When Clammy telephoned the next morning to ask Beth if she would ride Josie's Babe while he worked out Charmin', she made an excuse. Maybe in a little while it wouldn't hurt so much and she could do it, but she wasn't ready yet. She couldn't even stand the thought of being there when he came to pick up the horse.

She went out to do the morning feeding. It had looked like rain the night before, so the horses spent the night in their stalls. She measured out the grain and dumped some in each of their bins, then stood in Charmin's stall, watching him eat. He got a mouthful of oats and turned his head to look at her while he chewed. If only he belonged to her, she thought longingly. Charmin' turned back to the bin and snuffled up more grain.

Bang! Somewhere in the barn a door had closed sharply. She walked out of the stall. "Sophie?"

No one answered.

"Mom?" Beth raised her voice. She looked around. The barn was dim and empty. "Is anybody here?"

Careful not to make any noise, she moved toward the front. The door that led into the old cow stalls stood ajar. For some reason the back of her neck felt prickly. She hesitated for a moment, conscious of the silence, which seemed charged, menacing. She pushed the door open and peered in. There was a row of empty stanchions. Nothing moved. She walked down the row. A board creaked under her sneakered feet, and she jumped. At the far end of the row was a calf pen. As she looked inside, she felt a scratching on her ankle and screamed. A little field mouse, terrified by the noise, ran across the floor.

"Idiot!" Beth scolded herself.

There was no one in the barn. She must have been hearing things. She went back and checked the door between the barn and the passageway to the screened porch and farmhouse. It was closed—just as she'd left it.

Clop. Clop. Clop. She heard the hollow metallic sound of horses' hooves on the cement floor of the barn. Beth hurried back. Dolly was loose in the middle of the barn. It didn't make sense. The stall door opened inward. Beth felt the back of her neck get prickly. She looked around. The area under the haymow was shadowed and dark. She forced herself to walk over there, holding her breath. There was no one there. Charmin' whinnied shrilly, and she jumped.

This is ridiculous, she scolded herself. There was no reason for anyone to be in the barn. She caught hold of Dolly's halter. "How'd you manage to get out of your stall?" Her voice sounded loud in the empty barn. Dolly nuzzled her shoulder. "Come on. I'll let you out."

She took the little filly to the back door that led to the lane. The door was unbarred. She was sure she had locked it the previous night. There could have been someone in the barn! Someone who had slipped out while she was looking in the cows' stalls. Charmin' whinned again. "Hush, boy," Beth said.

How would someone have gotten in to begin with? She hurried to the front of the barn, remembering that she hadn't checked the doors. They were locked! There was no way anyone could have come in. It had to be her imagination, she told herself firmly. Dolly was waiting patiently at the back door and Beth returned to push it open. Then she heard the sound of Clammy's pickup pulling into the driveway. She let herself out into the lane, swung over the outside gate, and ran up the hill into the meadow.

It wasn't that she blamed Clammy. His hopes had been riding on this race a lot longer than hers, and he was more experienced. It all made sense. But sense didn't matter. It hurt too much when she thought of Charmin' racing without her.

The grass in the meadow was long, and the dew wet

her ankles. Wildflowers were moist and sparkly. Honeysuckle grew over the remains of a dilapidated wooden fence and gave off a sweet, heavy smell. She started to go closer to pick a branch but backed off when she saw the bees that had gotten there first.

Once past the meadow, she was no longer on Pretty Penny Farm property. She hopped a little ditch and walked to the field near the top of Pumpkin Hill Road. This was where Clammy had seen her on Charmin' for the first time and had stopped to ask her to ride with him. Forget about that, she told herself, picking up a small stone and skimming it across the hay stubble.

Ahead where the road curved to the left was a narrower, rutted road that went straight. She followed it and found herself going down the other side of the hill. She passed a small farmhouse where two black-and-white cows and a goat grazed behind a barbed-wire fence. Another half mile of walking, and she came to an old cemetery. There were woods all around it, and ancient pine trees were dotted among the gravestones. The stone wall in front was uneven and caved-in in places. Beth walked through an opening and looked at the stones.

What stories they had to tell. Jeremiah Hobson had died in 1821 at the age of seventy-two. He'd seen the Revolutionary War and the War of 1812. He'd also seen two wives, three daughters, and a son and grandson die before he did. One wife, Rebecca, had died in her twenties; the other, Maude, had lived until thirty-nine.

Some of the oldest gravestones had fallen backward. Beth leaned down to read one. It marked the grave of a mother and daughter and gave the same date of death, March 11, 1860. At the very bottom, however, there was a correction. *Nota Bene: The mother died in 1859.* Evidently the carver had made a mistake and, instead of making a new stone, had corrected it on the original. Some of the markers were simply small rectangular slabs in the ground. This was particularly true of the graves of young children. What calamity had struck the Lockharts, Beth wondered. Three children had died within one year.

Some of the thin, rust-colored slabs carried messages. Most had to do with hopes for an afterlife. Thomas Dobson's declared: "He is not dead, just asleep." Raymond Littlejohn, on the other hand, must have been a cynic, for his read: "As you are now, so once was I. As now I am, so shall you be." Beth felt a little chill pass over her. All these people had walked here once. Who was left to mourn them?

Ruff. Ruff. Ruff. Beth heard the labrador before he and Sarah Wentworth turned into the graveyard. The dog ran up to her, tail wagging.

"Hi, Freddy. How are you, boy?" Beth scratched his head.

"Good morning," Sarah greeted her. "You found our old graveyard, I see."

"Good morning, Mrs. Wentworth. I've been reading some of the headstones," Beth answered.

"Kinda curious, aren't they." Sarah smiled and sat down on the stone wall. "Freddy and I take a walk every nice day, and we like to come up here now and again. Makes all those little problems that seem so big 'pear kinda small."

"I was just wondering if there were still relatives of the people buried here who come visit the graves," Beth said.

"Hasn't been anyone buried here in this century, so I don't expect anyone comes to pay respects to the dead. Most likely they come to think of the living."

"It's very peaceful here. Quiet except for the birds. But it gives me sort of a . . . I don't know . . . an odd feeling."

"There's being alone, and there's being lonely. Maybe that's what you sense here. We're all going to be alone someday, but we don't have to be lonely in life even when we're by ourselves."

Freddy perked up his ears, raised his head, and then bounded out the gate and across the road. Sarah Wentworth laughed. "Must be a squirrel," she said. "Nothing stirs him up like that except for squirrels. They always get away, thank goodness, but he keeps chasin' them anyway. Just like some folks. Always have their eyes on something they can't have. Well"— she got up—"I set some bread to rise. Should be about ready by the time I get back. Maybe you'd like to stop by later and have some?"

"Sounds great," Beth said. "I guess I ought to go back, too. My mother could use some help in the garden."

Freddy came straggling from the brush at Sarah's whistles, and they walked back up the hill. At the top, they stopped to admire the view of the mountains. When they came to the meadow above the farm, Beth saw Sophie at the far side picking wildflowers. She said good-bye to Sarah and Freddy and went over to her.

"Clammy's gone, right?" she asked.

Sophie nodded. "I'm sorry about the race, Beth," she said shyly.

"Yeah." Beth leaned down and picked a fuzzy red flower.

"Clammy had a hard time getting Charmin' into the trailer." Sophie looked at her sympathetically. "I was hoping he wouldn't be able to."

"Thanks for the thought. I want Charmin' to run the race, though, even if I can't." Beth did not really want to talk about it. "There are so many wildflowers here. You never see anything like this at home." She picked a round lacy white blossom. "I know this one."

"Queen Anne's lace. It's a kind of carrot. See." Sophie pulled up a plant to show a thick yellow-orange root.

"Can you eat it?" Beth asked.

"No. My father says it's not good to eat."

"What is this yellow flower, do you know?"

Sophie frowned. "I think it's called galax. I haven't seen it often. I was just going to walk down in the woods. Wildflowers like woods, especially if they're a little wet. Want to come?"

"Sure," Beth agreed. She'd do anything to keep her mind off Clammy and Charmin'.

The two girls left the meadow and followed a trail in the woods. "Look at these." Beth darted off the path to pick a small clump of delicate purple flowers.

"Those are Quaker-ladies, but don't ask me why they're called that. Maybe because they look so shy and innocent." Sophie smiled. "That's one of the first wildflowers I remember."

"How'd you learn so much about them?" Beth asked. "Buffalo's a big city, right?"

"Sundays when I was little we always took rides in the country. In the spring and summer we would hunt for wildflowers and mushrooms. Look!" She ran down the trail. "This is my favorite in the whole world."

The flower looked like yellow wax. "That's unreal," Beth said. "It looks like an orchid or something."

"It's a lady-slipper." Sophie beamed. "See? The petals look like a slipper or moccasin. Isn't it wonderful?"

"It's one of the prettiest flowers I've ever seen." Beth touched the petal lightly.

"I feel so lucky we found it. But I'm not going to pick it. It would die quickly." Sophie crouched down close to the plant. "These were my mother's favorites. The few days we found them she would be very happy. She would never pick them either. She said they should be left to grace the woods."

"She must have been a gentle person—like you are," Beth said quietly.

"She was wonderful. So pretty. Little, not fat like me. And her hair was blond—almost white—and shiny. She was only twenty-five when she died. She should have been left to grace the world." Sophie seemed almost to be talking to herself. "We went on our Sunday trips afterward, but for a long time it was not really good. My father would get quiet and sad. Sometimes he would even cry if he thought I couldn't see him." She sighed, a shuddery sound. "Oh, well," she said, straightening up. "That was a long time ago. I never talked about it before. I guess it was the flower that brought it back. I haven't seen one in many, many years."

She sounded embarrassed and apologetic. Beth wanted to cry for the little girl and the sad man picking flowers in the woods. "It's all right to talk about it, Sophie. It must have been just awful to lose your mom when you were so little."

"The worst part is they didn't tell me." Sophie retreated again into the past.

"Didn't tell you?"

"They didn't tell me when she had died. They sent me to stay at my aunt's house. When I came home, she . . . my mother . . . wasn't there. My father said she'd gone away. She loved me, he said, but she'd had to go away. God wanted her. I didn't understand. I thought God had made her live somewhere else. I thought I'd been bad, and he had made her go away."

"That's terrible." Beth couldn't imagine anything worse.

"I used to pray every night he'd let her come back. I remember that Christmas I had tried very hard to be good. One of my aunts took me to see the Santa Claus in a store, and he kept asking me what I wanted for Christmas. I wouldn't tell him. He showed me a doll and a cradle and a rocking horse. I just kept shaking my head. I was sitting on his lap. He told me to whisper in his ear what I wanted. I whispered, 'Mama.' He asked me where she was. I told him with God. Then I saw these big tears in his eyes, and I jumped down and ran away. I thought I must be so bad not even Santa Claus could give me what I wanted."

"What did your aunt do?"

"She ran after me, but I wouldn't tell her what happened. I was too ashamed."

"I don't understand why your family didn't tell you," Beth said.

"I don't know. They never talked about it in front of me. Whenever they mentioned my mother, it was just reminiscing. The word 'death' was never used. They are all religious. Roman Catholic. They believe in an afterlife and all that."

"When did you find out?"

"Not for a year, when I was in first grade. We kept gerbils in a cage. One morning we came in and one of them was lying there cold and stiff. Everybody was crying, and the nun said not to cry; it had gone to animal heaven to be with God. Then I knew."

Beth didn't know what to say. She could picture the child standing there, looking at the dead animal, seeing her dead mother. She felt her eyes smarting and looked down.

"Beth . . ." Sophie looked at her, surprised. "You're crying for me. Don't feel bad."

"I am so sorry. I don't know what to say." Beth rubbed her eyes.

"I don't know why I told you. I never told anyone before, not even my father. I didn't mean to make you sad. Here you are so disappointed about Charmin', and I have to go and tell you old troubles. Come on." She started down the path. "Let's see what other flowers we can find."

What a morning it had been, Beth thought as they walked together through the woods. She had run away from her disappointment to the graveyard, where dreams had died long ago, then to Sophie, whose buried pain had risen with a flower. Sophie was brave. Sarah Wentworth was wise. Beth Bridgewater was neither. But she was learning. She would go to the fairground with Clammy tomorrow, and she would ride Josie's Babe. She could not be in the race, but she could be part of it.

"I'm going back," she told Sophie. "I want to be there when Clammy gets home."

"Wait a minute. Look." Sophie pointed to a cluster of tall flowers. "They're jack-in-the-pulpits," she said. "See the preacher and the pulpit."

There was a greenish-yellow flower on a long stalk,

surrounded by a trumpetlike green leaf that was striped brown and purple. It did look like a minister in a pulpit. "That's neat!" Beth leaned down to get a better look.

"It's also called Indian turnip. I don't want to pull one up to show you, but the root looks like a turnip. My father used to make cough medicine out of the juice." Sophie made a face.

"Did it work?" Beth asked.

"My father thought so. Tasted terrible, however." She handed Beth the flowers she had gathered. "Will you put these in water when you get back?"

"Sure." Beth took them. "And I'd love to come looking for flowers with you another day. You know so much about them."

"I wish it were spring. There are lots more then." Sophie looked pleased at the compliment.

"See you later."

Beth turned to walk away. She liked Sophie—really liked her. It was hard to deal with; confusing. She thought of those last days in school: her perception of Sophie as a wimp, her willingness to humiliate Sophie in order to distance herself from her. It made her cringe to think about it. Sophie had a lot going for her, and she was willing to share her talents. Amy had used her because she was a good writer. And she, Beth, had used her because she was a good listener. She had taken without giving anything back. She turned around.

"Hey, Sophie," she called. "You teach me to square-dance and recognize wildflowers, and I'll teach you to ride Dolly. A deal?"

Sophie waved and grinned. "Sure. It's a deal."

Beth jogged back through the meadow, then across the front lawn to the side of the house. Out of breath, she plopped down on the porch step. She didn't hear anyone come up behind her, and was startled when hands were clamped over her eyes. "Mom?"

"No." The voice was falsetto.

Beth reached up and tried to pull the hands away. "Who is it?"

There was a giggle, and the hands dropped from her eyes. "Surprise." Amy leaned over her, laughing.

"Amy! I don't believe it!" Beth had the funniest feeling in the pit of her stomach. She should be really happy to see her best friend, but she wasn't.

"Mom and my sister, Laura, are going up to visit Dartmouth," Amy explained. "Laura would love to go to a jock school, you know. I didn't want to hang around up there, so I had them drop me off to spend the day with you."

"Great," Beth lied.

"I thought you'd be glad to see somebody besides Bouncing Boobs. Has it been just awful?" Amy asked.

"Not really." Beth looked at the flowers in her hand. "Come on in the house. I have to put these in some water."

"I hope they don't give me hay fever." Amy followed her into the house. "I'm allergic to weeds."

"They're not weeds. They're wildflowers." Beth hunted around in the cupboard for a vase. "So how's your summer been? How's the gang?"

"It's been hot. You've missed some good parties. We spent last Saturday night at the reservoir with a keg. Got chased by the cops. Tory was so drunk she almost fell in. I did my 'But, Officer, we're just innocent kids' routine. They bought it and let us stay."

"Sounds wild. Who was there? Just the three of you?" Beth settled for a pewter pitcher.

"Are you kidding? Three of us with a keg? There were some guys from the swim team. Tommy Norris and Greg Albert—he's really a hunk—and Johnny Bertino."

"And your mothers let you go?" Beth immediately regretted the question.

"This country air must have softened your brain." Amy laughed. "We told them we were staying at each other's houses, of course."

"Oh." That was all Beth could manage.

"What do you do around here for excitement?" Amy opened the refrigerator and helped herself to a diet soda. "Have you met any guys?"

"Well..." Beth hesitated. She was dying to talk about Dave, but something warned her not to. She decided to ignore the last question. "There are square dances at the Grange every Saturday night. They're fun."

"Square dances? This is really the woods. Are they all farmers that go?"

"Not all." Beth couldn't resist. "There are some college guys around. I've met one from the University of Virginia."

"What's he doing up here?" Amy swung up onto the counter and sat cross-legged.

"He comes from here. His father has a horse camp."

"How'd you meet him?"

"Well, his father is caretaker for Pretty Penny Farm. They keep some horses here."

Amy wrinkled her nose. "Oh."

"They're really nice people." Beth felt she had to defend the Fullers from Amy's snobbishness. She heard a car pulling into the driveway and went to the window. "Excuse me a minute, will you? Clammy's here with my horse. Be right back."

"*Clammy?* What a name. Is that your boyfriend?" Amy ran to the window to get a look.

"No." It seemed impossible to explain it all to Amy. It was as if they were shouting from opposite shores of a wide river and neither one could really hear the other. "He's a kid I ride with." She went out the door.

Amy followed her out. "Did you say your horse? Did you buy one?"

Beth shook her head. "Leased him."

"Brought him back good and sound," Clammy said, opening the trailer.

"How'd it go?" Beth asked, trying to sound matter-of-fact.

" 'Bout what you'd expect." Clammy backed Charmin' down the ramp. "We had a little go-round 'bout who was boss, and I'm not sure the hoss didn't win. Ayeh. He let me know he wouldn't give me anything for nothing."

"How was his time today?"

"Nowhere near what he did for you, but he'll stop sulking and get used to me."

"I'll take him in and clean him up, Clammy." Beth took the horse's bridle, and he nuzzled her shoulder.

"What a beautiful horse!" Amy came over. "Can I ride him, Beth?"

That was the last thing Beth wanted. She was trying to think of an excuse, but Clammy saved her. "He's prob'ly been worked enough for one day. He's getting ready for a race in a little over a week," he explained. "Shouldn't be ridden just for pleasure."

"Oh? Do you own him?" Amy asked.

"No. This is Clammy Ellis." Beth performed belated introductions. "He's riding him for the Fullers. This is my friend from home, Amy Staples."

Clammy nodded to her. "Hi. Say, Beth, saw those dudes again from Rockingham. Charmin' didn't show them anything to worry about today."

"I thought you said you leased the horse," Amy said to Beth. "What's the good of leasing a horse if you can't ride him?"

"It's complicated. I'll explain it later. I'll ride Josie's Babe with you tomorrow," Beth said to Clammy.

"That will be a real help. Sure appreciate it." He walked around and opened the door on the driver's side. "See you in the morning."

"I hope that's not one of these great college guys you've been raving about," Amy said as he backed out. " 'Ayeh,' " she mocked his accent. "Have you tried fixing him up with Sophie? They'd make a cute couple."

Had Amy always been this mean, Beth wondered, or did it just seem more obvious here on the farm? She didn't belong here, that was certain, and Beth wished she had never come.

"Beth, quick, where's your mother?" Sophie rushed into the kitchen, her eyes wide.

Beth pointed to a note on the refrigerator. "At the store. What's the matter, Sophie?"

"There are some men out back, and they're acting strange," Sophie said.

"Men? Where out back?" Beth started for the door.

"In the lane behind the barn. I'd just found a bunch of oyster mushrooms on a tree in the woods when this pickup truck came right across the field and parked in the bushes. I thought I was seeing things." Sophie put out her hand to stop Beth from going out the door. "I don't think you ought to go out there. We'd better wait for your mother."

"But what are they doing on our property?" Beth was indignant.

"I don't know, but they don't want to be seen, that's for sure," Sophie said. "They got out of the truck, and they cut through the woods—real close to me. I crouched down so they couldn't see me. I heard one of them say something about knowing a ringer when he saw one. It didn't make any sense. Anyway, they went into the lane. I followed to see what they were going to do."

"And?"

"They caught Charmin'."

Beth didn't wait to hear any more. She pushed past Sophie and ran out the door. "Wait!" Sophie yelled.

"Stay there if you're afraid," Beth called back. "I'm going to find out what they want."

Beth raced around the side of the barn and into the back meadow. She could hear Sophie running after her. There was no one in sight. She jumped over the fence into the lane and ran as fast as she could. "Charmin'!" she yelled.

"Beth! Beth!" Sophie was calling way behind her, but she didn't stop. What if they had done something to Charmin'? She reached the crest of the slope and looked down the lane. There he was, standing under a tree, gazing up at her. Dolly lifted her head from grazing, whinnied, and trotted toward her. There were no men. Shaking with relief, she turned around. Sophie, perspiring from running and out of breath, was holding her stomach and pointing to the field on the other side. A red pickup was backing fast into the road. Tires screeched, dust flew, and it drove off.

"See? There they go," Sophie panted.

Something clicked. "I've seen that truck before," Beth said. "At the fairgrounds when I was working out with Charmin'. They must have followed Clammy!"

"What for?" Sophie was beginning to breathe normally.

Beth shook her head. "I don't know. Sophie, tell me everything you saw."

"There were two men. One held Charmin', and the other one looked him all over. He got down and ran his hands over each of his legs. Then he got up. He had something in his hand, but I couldn't see what it was. He rubbed it on Charmin's face. Charmin' tried to get away—he stood on his hind legs."

"You mean he reared?" Beth was shocked. That wasn't like Charmin'. He was high-strung, but she'd never seen him rear.

"That's when I ran to the house to get your mother."

"I've got to see if he's all right." Beth walked slowly toward Charmin'. She didn't want to startle him. He pricked up his ears, extended his neck, and took a few steps toward her. There were treats in her pocket as always, and she fumbled for the carrot. He crunched it noisily while she scratched behind his ear. When she put her face on his neck, it smelled funny. Like ammonia, but not exactly. Where had she smelled it before? Then it came to her. She associated it with painting. It was turpentine. Weird, but Charmin' seemed okay.

She heard her name called. Amy! She had been in

the bathroom when Sophie rushed in, and Beth had forgotten all about her.

Sophie looked at her, questioning. "Amy?" she asked in a dull voice.

"She's here for the day." Even to herself, Beth sounded apologetic. "We'd better go back. I have to call Dave and tell him what you saw." She took off at a run.

"Where'd you disappear to?" Amy asked as Beth came into the house, the screen door slamming behind her.

Beth held up her hand. "Later." She grabbed the phone and dialed. Luckily, Dave answered right away. "You've got to come over here. Some men have been fooling around with Charmin'! Can you come right away?"

Beth hung up the phone. "Whew. Dave's on his way," she told Sophie, who was standing in the doorway.

"You mind telling me what's going on?" Amy sounded piqued.

"I don't know. Some men were fooling around with the horses. Sophie saw them."

"Oh, hi, Sophie." Amy smiled sweetly. "What were they doing? And who's this Dave?"

"We don't know what they were doing," Beth answered. "Dave owns Charmin'."

"My, my, my," Amy teased, "a mystery at Pretty Penny Farm. I'm so glad I got here for it."

"It's not funny," Beth said.

"Your mother's pulling into the driveway." Sophie was still at the door. "She'll know what to do."

"Aren't you even going to say hello to me, Sophie?" Amy asked.

"Hello, Amy." Sophie opened the door so Beth could go out to meet her mother.

Elinor was not out of the car before Beth started telling her the story.

"Take it easy, sweetheart," she said, pulling out a package with one hand, then putting her other arm around Beth.

Amy and Sophie had come outside, and Elinor looked up in surprise. "Amy Staples!" she said. "How in the world did you get here?"

"Hi, Mrs. Bridgewater. I'm *so* glad to see you again. I hope you don't mind my popping in for the day. My mother and Laura are looking at Dartmouth."

"Oh. The day. Of course not. Now, honey." She squeezed Beth. "Calm down and tell me what happened."

Beth and Sophie repeated their story. Elinor Bridgewater thought they should report it to the police, but Beth insisted they wait for Dave. He was not long in coming.

"Wow," Amy whispered to Beth when he got out of the Jeep, "now, *he's* a hunk! Introduce me."

Beth tried not to sound irritated as she made the introductions. "This is Amy, a friend from home. This is Dave Fuller. Like I told you, he owns Charmin'."

Amy held out her hand. "I'm *really* glad to meet you," she said, smiling.

Dave shook her hand, but he was looking at Beth. "You sounded pretty upset on the phone," he said. "Let's hear about it."

"Tell what you saw, Sophie." Beth noticed that Amy had finally let go of Dave's fingers.

Sophie went over the details for the third time. Then Beth told him about the smell. "Why would they rub turpentine on Charmin'?" she asked.

"How would I know?" Dave sounded irritated, and Beth looked at him in surprise. "Sorry," he said, "I didn't mean to yell at you. Sophie, what did these guys look like?"

"I couldn't see them very well," Sophie replied. "One was tall, and he looked younger than the other one. He was short and sort of heavy—the older man."

"They had a red pickup," Beth told him, "and I think I've seen it before at the fairgrounds when I was there with Clammy."

Dave slammed his fist into his hand. "This is my pig-headed father's fault!"

"Dave," Elinor admonished, "you shouldn't talk about your dad like that."

"Right," he muttered, "but if he weren't so darned stubborn . . ."

"I don't see what you're getting at." Beth stared at him, confused.

"Just drop it. Okay?" He pounded his palm in nervous little jerks.

"I think we should report this to the sheriff." Elinor half turned to go into the house.

"No way. Absolutely no way!" Dave's voice was loud.

Amy spoke up. "I think Mrs. Bridgewater is right." Beth felt like telling her to mind her own business.

"This is private property, and they were trespassing," Elinor insisted.

"This isn't a suburb," Dave said. "People here cross property lines all the time. Cows get out. You go get them. As long as you don't do any damage, nobody here would call it a crime."

"But they weren't here after any cows," Beth said. "For all we know, they might have been going to steal Charmin'."

"But you don't know that, and they didn't steal anything. What are you going to tell the sheriff? Two men came into your pasture and looked at a horse and now the horse smells funny? He'd be too polite to laugh in your face, but he'd feel like it, and he'd spread the story around."

"I don't get you, Dave." Beth felt her face getting red. He was treating her so badly in front of Amy. "You act all upset, and then when Mom wants to call the police, you practically tell us we're acting like some kind of dumb city people who don't know the score."

"I'm sorry," he said, his tone softer. "I didn't mean it that way. I just want to handle this myself. I'll keep an eye on the place. That okay, Mrs. Bridgewater?"

Elinor shrugged and looked at Beth. "What do you say, honey? I guess we don't have much to go on."

"And when I'm not around, Beth, you can just call me if you see anything at all out of the way." He didn't wait for an answer. "I'm going up and take a look at the horses."

"Do you mind if I come?" Amy smiled. "I haven't even seen the other horse."

"No!" Beth snapped. "I mean, let Dave go by himself. Charmin's had enough strangers pawing him for one morning."

"I'd hardly paw him." Amy gave Beth a look.

"Maybe you'd have some lunch with us?" Elinor asked.

"No thank you, I should get back home," Dave answered.

"Who knows? If you stay, maybe those men will come back." Amy was obviously teasing. And flirting. Beth was furious.

Dave didn't answer. "See you later," he said, heading out past the barn.

"Well, we'd better see what we can put together in the kitchen. Want to give me a hand, girls?" Elinor suggested.

"I forgot the mushrooms!" Sophie exclaimed. "Wait until you see them, Mrs. B."

Beth and Amy followed Elinor into the house. "Tell me more about this Dave." Amy poked Beth.

"He's okay. He's a nice guy, that's all."

"Just a nice guy, huh? He's the one from the University of Virginia, right?"

"Yeah."

"So is he your boyfriend, or what?"

"No." Beth changed the subject. "What do you want me to do?" she asked her mother.

"I'll bet you've got the hots for him," Amy said softly.

"Why don't you cut up some tomatoes. There are black olives and feta cheese in the fridge. We'll have a nice Greek salad."

"I'd be glad to help, too," Amy volunteered.

"Fine, Amy. There's iced tea mix in the pantry, and lemons in a basket on the counter." Elinor took a ham from the refrigerator. "How are things at home? Have you had a nice summer?"

"Oh, yes, thank you. I've just been doing the usual stuff—sailing, swimming, playing tennis. Getting in shape before the school year. I expect I'll have to study awfully hard in high school."

"Swimming in the reservoir, you said." Beth couldn't resist. She hated Amy putting on the wholesome act for her mother.

"Is that allowed?" Elinor asked.

"Well, I only did it once on a dare. I usually swim at the club. What are *those?*" Amy pointed at the basket that Sophie was bringing in.

"Sophie, what a bonanza!" Elinor took them from her. "Wait until you taste these oyster mushrooms, Amy. They'll melt in your mouth."

"Hey, Sophie, you look different. Have you lost weight?" Amy asked.

"You've lost about twelve pounds, right?" Beth said encouragingly.

"Twelve and a half," Sophie answered. "But I have about twenty to go."

"You'll do it before the summer's over," Elinor encouraged. "You've certainly shown you have the will-power."

"You really do look different." Amy looked her over again. "It's not just the weight. I can't quite figure out what it is."

Sophie blushed as Amy stared at her, a slight smile on her face and one eyebrow raised. "I don't remember seeing you in jeans before. Maybe that's it. I always think of you in skirts . . . very full skirts. Didn't you always wear them?" Amy asked.

Sophie looked down and shrugged.

Beth could see that Sophie knew she was being teased. Elinor had taken her shopping and had outfit-ted her with bras, blue jeans, and T-shirts. Sophie had been thrilled to be dressed finally in the suburban teenager uniform. Now she looked self-conscious and awkward.

"Do you think it's the jeans, Beth? Is that why Sophie looks different?" Amy persisted, winking at Beth.

"I don't know." Beth tried to change the subject. "I like your new haircut, Amy." Amy had dark brown hair, which she had had cut short, and it curled all over her head.

"Thanks." Amy would not be deterred. "I think I've got it! Sophie used to have something sort of bouncy about her. Now she's just . . . well . . . more . . ."

Beth gave Amy a warning look. It didn't matter that her mother and Sophie wouldn't get the reference to "Bouncing Boobs." Amy was just going too far. "Did you get the ice for the tea, Amy?" she interrupted. "There's a plastic container in the back of the freezer." How was she going to stand the rest of the day torn between the two of them? She felt she had to protect Sophie from Amy's barbs, but she wasn't ready to alienate her old friend.

After they'd finished, she agreed to take Amy out to see the horses in the pasture.

"I don't see why we can't ride them," Amy complained.

"You can ride Dolly. I told you that," Beth said.

"By myself? That's no fun." Amy looked sulky.

"I'm really sorry, Amy, but Charmin' shouldn't be pleasure-ridden. I told you he's racing in two weeks."

"I don't see what harm it would do," Amy persisted. "Are we just going to hang around here all afternoon? We'll be stuck with Sophie, too, I suppose. I almost wish I'd gone to Dartmouth."

Beth wished she had, too, but she couldn't say that, of course. What could they do for the afternoon? She certainly didn't want to spend any more time with Amy and Sophie together. If she were careful not to tire Charmin', maybe it wouldn't hurt to go for a ride.

"We'll go for a trail ride if you want to so much," she said finally. "Bring Dolly."

"You sure you don't mind?" Amy took hold of Dolly's bridle.

"We just won't ride them hard, okay?" Beth led Charmin' toward the lane.

"Anything you say." Amy grinned.

They were brushing the horses when Beth heard her mother calling her. She sounded upset. Beth hurried through the passageway to the screened porch.

"Look at this!" Elinor was at a window examining the screen. Three edges of it were loose. "Do you have any idea how this could have happened?"

Beth walked over and looked. The screen had been cut. "No." She shook her head. "Why would anyone cut the screen?"

"I can't imagine," her mother said. "There's nothing on this porch to steal."

"Unless someone were trying to break into the house. Mom, do you think it was a robber?"

"I don't know what to think." Elinor looked worried. "The connecting door is locked, so there's really no way to get in. This gives access to the barn. Is there anything missing out there ... saddles or anything?"

"No. Everything's there, but wait. ..." Beth remembered the noises she'd heard in the barn earlier. "Something did happen while I was feeding the horses." She explained the events of the morning. "I didn't think much about it then, but do you suppose I surprised someone out there?"

"It certainly sounds like it. I tell you, I just can't get over this. I thought we were getting away from vandalism and suburban crime. It makes me mad to think about it."

"What are you going to do?" Beth asked.

"Well, I'll call the sheriff and report it. Then I'd best get this screen fixed. We'll keep the doors locked at all times. Good thing your father's coming for his vacation tomorrow."

"Yeah," Beth agreed. It was scary to think of someone prowling around out in the barn when she had thought she was alone. "We were going for a ride, but do you want me to hang around?"

"No, go for your ride, dear. I'll speak to the sheriff."

Beth went back and saddled the horses. Amy had not ridden much, but she was comfortable around animals and naturally athletic. They walked the horses down Pumpkin Hill Road, riding abreast except when an occasional car passed by. Then they hugged the edge of the narrow dirt road.

"Idiot!" Beth yelled at a car that came close and fast, spewing stones from under its tires and startling the horses, who started to run. "Whoa, Charmin'. Easy, boy," she soothed. She pulled back on the reins, petting the horse's neck at the same time. Charmin' responded and quieted down. Dolly, who was behind, followed his lead.

Half a mile below Sarah Wentworth's farm, they turned into the woods and trotted along easily on a wide snowmobile trail. It was fun having someone to ride with, and the woods were still and beautiful. Beth was happy she had given in to Amy. Her misgivings seemed silly, and it was a relief to be away from the tension she had felt at lunch.

"Isn't it beautiful here?" she asked Amy. "I think I could live on a farm."

"Not me." Amy laughed. "It's okay to visit, but I'd be bored in a week."

"Probably you would." Beth didn't resent Amy's attitude. It was the truth. Amy had to be the center of activities, had to have action all the time.

"What do you do when you're not riding? A square dance once a week isn't exactly my idea of exciting. Besides, you're saddled with Sophie. Isn't that a pain?"

There was no nastiness in Amy's tone. It seemed to be a sincere question. Beth remembered she had felt much the same way back in Riverdale. "She's not a bad kid when you get to know her," she said.

"Really? She seems like such a lump. I can't imagine bothering to get to know her."

And that was the truth, too. To Amy, if someone wasn't pretty, athletic, and popular, you didn't bother getting to know them . . . unless, of course, they could do something for you. That was just the way she was, and Beth guessed she couldn't help it.

"Sophie's had a pretty unhappy life." She thought about Sophie and the story she had told about her mother dying. That wasn't something she could share with Amy.

"You sound as if you really like her. Course you'll

have to drop her when you get back home. My brother says at the high school if you don't hang out with the jocks, you're nowhere."

"I'm not exactly a jock myself," Beth said.

"The guys we've been going out with on the swim team are. I'll fix you up when you get back. That'll get you in."

Beth thought about Dave. She wasn't sure she was going to want to go out with some guy on the swim team. This was probably silly of her. If everything worked out for him, he'd be at U.Va., and she'd be the last person he'd be thinking of.

"Let's follow that path." Amy pointed to her right, then turned Dolly onto the path, urging her to go faster as she did so.

Beth was caught off guard. "Wait up!" she called, but Dolly had broken into a canter.

"This is fun," Amy called over her shoulder. "Try and catch us!"

Beth did not want to canter. The trail was rough and looked little used. Charmin', annoyed at having Dolly in front, strained at the bit. "Dumb!" she muttered. The trail wound around, and Dolly and Amy were out of sight. She relaxed her grip and let Charmin' break into a canter. Then she held him back. She ducked to avoid a branch and felt the leaves slap across her face. A large tree lay angled across the path in front of her. Charmin' did not hesitate but cleared it easily. After they rounded the curve, the trail got steeper. Through the trees she caught a glimpse of Amy's red shirt up the hill ahead of her. It disappeared quickly from view. She must have little Dolly in a full gallop, which was a stupid thing to do. A rock clattered as her horse dislodged it. An overhanging bush scratched at her jeans. Charmin' was fighting the bit again, anxious to overtake the mare. She pulled back hard and felt her left hand jerk back and hit her shoulder. The rein had broken.

No. No. *No.*

When the colt felt the pressure released, he surged forward. Beth didn't know what to do. Pulling too hard on the right rein would confuse him. She was leaning forward, hanging on to his mane. "Whoa, Charmin', whoa!" she begged. He was going as fast as he had on the fairground track. Here it was not exhilarating—it was terrifying. "Please, Charmin', please. Whoa!"

Now she could see Dolly and Amy in front of them. "Stop, Amy! Stop!" she yelled desperately.

Amy turned around, laughing.

"Stop!"

Amy finally seemed to realize something was wrong. She started to slow Dolly as Charmin', smashing into the brush on the side, surged past, knocking against the mare.

The impact slowed Charmin'. "Whoa, Charmin', whoa," Beth urged. There was a small natural clearing just ahead. She put pressure on the right rein as they approached. He turned and dropped back to a trot. "That's it, boy, whoa." She pulled again, and he stopped. Trembling all over, Beth slid to the ground.

She did not feel as if her legs would hold her. She reached out and hung on to the bridle. Was Amy all right? She turned to look back as a frightened-looking Amy trotted up.

"What happened?" Amy asked.

"My rein broke. He bolted." Beth could hardly talk. Her teeth were chattering.

"Ohhh. I'm sorry. I thought you were just trying to beat me when you yelled to stop. I'm really sorry." Amy looked pale under her tan.

"We could have been really hurt, you know." It was all Amy's fault for cantering, and Beth was angry.

"I didn't know your rein had broken. How could I?" Amy got defensive.

"You never should have galloped on a trail like this." Beth rubbed her sleeve across her sweaty face.

"I said I was sorry. You're not hurt, are you?"

"No. I'm all right, just shook up, that's all." She tugged on Charmin's bridle. "Come on, boy. I'll have to walk you back."

Going back down the steep slope was tricky. Beth guided the horse carefully, but even so, his back leg slipped in one particularly steep area of shale, and she was almost knocked off balance. She was grateful when they got back to the snowmobile trail.

"Is he limping?" Amy was behind her on Dolly.

"I don't think so," Beth answered, turning to face Charmin' so she could watch his movements.

"I think he's favoring his right back leg," Amy said.

She was right. It wasn't a pronounced limp, more

like a hesitation as he put that hoof down. Beth's first thought was that he might have a small stone lodged there. She had Amy hold him while she examined the hoof. She couldn't see anything, but he seemed to get worse as they went along. "He really is limping now." Beth's voice was tense with worry.

Amy tried to reassure her. "I think he's walking about the same."

"What if I've ruined him for the race?" Beth bit her lip. It was such a horrible idea. "Mr. Fuller will never forgive me." And Dave. What would Dave think of her? How stupid she had been to take him out. She had known better, and if she hadn't, Clammy had certainly warned her.

They had just turned onto Pumpkin Hill Road when she heard a car behind them. She pulled Charmin' off to the side. It was Dave in the Fullers' Jeep. He stopped and came over. "Look what I've done!" Beth blurted out. "Charmin's limping."

"Take it easy, Beth." Dave squeezed her shoulder. "Let's have a look." He picked up Charmin's leg and examined the hoof, then he ran his hands down the leg. "It can't be too serious," he said. "Probably just a muscle or a tendon. What happened?"

Beth told him about the rein breaking and the horse bolting. "It's all my fault," she concluded. "I never should have taken him on the trail."

"Let's get him back to the farm," Dave said. "I'll go on ahead and call the vet. He only lives a couple of miles from here. If we're lucky, we'll catch him at home." He smiled at Amy as he patted Beth's shoulder.

He was so nice to her. She couldn't understand why he wasn't angry. She was furious with herself. All the way up the road she pictured the vet saying Charmin' was ruined for life. Her guilt and remorse called forth visions of someone shooting the wonderful horse. By the time they reached the farm, she was in tears.

It was half an hour before the vet arrived. Beth couldn't talk, not even to Dave—especially not to Dave, no matter how sweet he was being. It was obvious that she had done a wrong thing and the consequences were really serious. She sat rigid and miserable while Amy chatted on to him about the University of Virginia.

Finally a panel truck pulled into the drive. It was the vet. Beth felt herself trembling as he carefully went over the horse.

"Heah's the problem," he said, indicating an area below the knee. "He's pulled a muscle. There's some swelling, and it's inflamed."

"What does that mean? Is he going to be all right?" Beth felt her eyes tear again.

"Sure," he answered. "I'll just bandage him up, and in about a couple of weeks he'll be good as new."

"Oh, thank you! Thank you!" Beth could have hugged him. Then she remembered. "The race—he's supposed to race August ninth."

"Don't know about that. Can't be worked till he's stopped limping. He goin' for the Pearson Prize at the fair?"

"He was," Dave answered. "But my father'll just have to enter another horse, wouldn't you say?"

"Don't know. He could be fine. Then again, after a layoff . . ."

"I think we'd be much safer not to count on him." Dave looked at Beth, who was the picture of misery, hands over her face. "Don't take it so hard, Beth. It's not a serious injury, and that's what counts."

"But your father . . ."

"He's got Josie's Babe, remember?"

"But if only I hadn't . . ."

"Stop blaming yourself. Accidents happen. He could have hurt himself in the pasture."

"But he didn't."

"Enough mea culpas, okay?"

He left soon after, and Beth was glad when Amy's mother and sister came to pick her up. She needed time alone to think. Her mother did not insist she eat supper when she saw how upset she was. Beth went right to her room, her mind going over and over the events of the afternoon. If she hadn't gone on the trail ride to please Amy, Charmin' wouldn't have been hurt. But then the rein would have given way at another point.

"Beth?"

Sophie was at the door.

"Yeah?" Beth answered.

"May I come in for a minute? I won't stay."

"Come in. It's not locked."

Sophie was holding a matted sketch in her hands. "I

was working on this to give you at the end of the summer," she said, "but then when you were so disappointed about the race, I hurried up and finished it today. It really isn't very good"—she held it out—"but I thought you might like it."

Beth looked down at the sketch in her hand. It was a pencil drawing of a girl on a horse. She and Charmin'. Neat lettering announced the title: *The Thoroughbreds.*

Beth couldn't understand Dave. He visited often the next week but did not seem to share her concern about Charmin'. When the limp disappeared after eight days, she ran to tell him the good news. She was excited, and the burden of guilt she had been carrying eased a bit. "The vet says he still can't be worked," she said, "but look at how much better he is." She led the way to the pasture. When Charmin' trotted up to them, running easily, Dave did not smile.

"Clammy's working Josie's Babe," he said. "That's the horse Dad intended to enter, and that's the horse he will enter."

"But, look," Beth protested. "Charmin' will be able to do it. Don't you see?"

"It was a crazy idea to begin with," Dave said, "and

now it would be even crazier. He could go lame on the track."

"Do you mean I've ruined him? Is that what you're saying?"

"Why do you take this so personally?" He sounded irritable. "He isn't going to run a race. It's no big deal. He's alive and well and grazing in the pasture. What more could a horse want?"

"You sound so bitter."

"Me? I couldn't be happier. I mean it, Beth. And if I sound otherwise, it's not directed at you. I promise. In fact, you've saved my life."

"What are you talking about?"

He looked up to see his father at the fence and waved to him.

"Well, he's lookin' better today." Percy Fuller swung over the top rail and went up to Charmin' in the pasture. He led him around by the halter, watching carefully as Charmin' moved. Then he came back toward them. "Hold him a minute, will you, Beth?" he said.

"Sure." She climbed over the fence and took the horse.

Mr. Fuller examined the sore leg. "He's not even actin' like it's tender," he said. "You must be taking right good care of him."

Beth said nothing. She was embarrassed by the compliment. Taking care of Charmin' was the least she could do.

"Startin' tomorrow," Mr. Fuller said, "I want you to

exercise him a bit on the lunge line. You ever worked with one?"

"Plenty of times," Beth said.

"Good. I think we've got a shot at this race yet."

Dave turned and left without a word.

Charmin' worked well on the lunge line, and three days before the race, the vet said he could be ridden again. Whether he could come up to form was another question.

Clammy did a light workout the first day back at the fairgrounds. Charmin' seemed glad to be back running. The next day Beth rode Josie's Babe. She was determined to be cheerful and to do all she could to help. Maybe she would earn the title Sophie had put on the picture.

In the workout, Charmin' equaled his best time: fifty-eight seconds. "We got us a winner." Clammy's freckled face was beaming. "We'll take any ringers they bring up!"

"I've been so worried that I might have ruined everything with that dumb trail ride," Beth said. "But now I know you're going to do it! I'm so happy."

"You're a good sport, Beth." This was high praise from a New Englander. "You notice when we came in, they were settin' up the carnival on the other side of the grounds. It'll open tonight. You want to go?"

Was he asking her for a date, Beth wondered. "Well . . ." she began slowly.

He grinned at her, seeming to read her mind. "I saw

Dave at the Fullers'. He's game. Told me to speak to you and Zosh."

Sophie had signed her sketch "Zascha," Polish for "Sophia" and the pen name she used. Beth loved the name and had shortened it to Zosh, realizing the nickname had something to do with the change in their relationship. She no longer seemed to Beth the klutzy, pudgy, unpopular Sophie. She was Zosh, the girl of the mushrooms and wildflowers.

"Sounds great," Beth said, blushing. Clammy had given her a sly look when he mentioned Dave.

"Let's cool 'em down and load 'em," Clammy said. "No sense in pushin'. Charmin's tuned just right."

They unsaddled and walked the horses on the track. When they came back to the stable area, there were a few people unloading horses. "Must be from Rockingham," Clammy said. "Bringing their horses to stable for the night."

"Hi, kids." Beth recognized the man called Al. Mr. Carl came around from behind the trailer. "Watched your workout," he said. "Looked pretty fast. What was your time?"

"Fair." Clammy was noncommittal.

"Looked from here like you might have broken a minute," Al said.

"Close to it, I guess." Clammy led Charmin' to the trailer.

Mr. Carl inspected the horse closely. "Where'd you come upon an animal like this?" he asked.

"Ain't mine. I'm riding him for a friend. Load the Babe, Beth," Clammy said.

"Where'd your friend get him? I might be interested in talking to him about buying."

"Name's Dave Fuller," Clammy said. "Don't think he'd be interested . . . least, not before the race." He followed Beth into the trailer. "Nosy fella," he whispered to her.

"Tell your friend I'll be looking for him tomorrow," Mr. Carl called as they were getting into the van.

That night, as they drove to the fairgrounds, Clammy repeated the conversation to Dave. "What's this guy look like?" Dave asked.

"He's 'bout fifty or so. Kinda short and squat. Gray hair and a little mustache," Clammy answered.

"He's not local, huh?"

"No way. I'd say New Yawk. Wouldn't you, Beth?" Clammy leaned forward to address Beth in the front seat.

"Definitely. And he's a pretty slick dresser. Every time he's been around, he's been wearing a suit," Beth said.

"Every time?" Dave looked at her. "You've seen him before?"

"Three or four times," she answered. "He's the guy who yelled to me the day your dad decided to race Charmin'. And . . ."

"And what?"

"He may be the one Sophie saw in the pasture. The pickup looked the same to me."

Dave was frowning. "That settles it!" he said abruptly. "Josie's Babe has to run tomorrow."

"Your father filled out the papers for Charmin' today," Clammy said. "Why, Dave, he'd 've been crazy not to. That hoss flies."

Dave said no more, but Beth could see he was upset. If these guys had been at the farm, it was creepy, but they hadn't come back, she reminded herself. And they hadn't hurt Charmin'.

Even though Dave took her on rides and won her a teddy bear at the duck shooting booth, he acted preoccupied and edgy all evening.

"Let's go on the Ferris wheel, Zosh," Clammy suggested. "Then we'd better call it a night. I've gotta be in shape for tomorrow."

Clammy and Zosh got in the first seat that came along. It swung back and forth after the attendant fastened the bar. "Don't make it rock." Zosh laughed. "I'll get seasick."

"We might as well ride, too." Dave held the bar of the next chair, then climbed in after Beth.

They were the last customers, and slowly the wheel lifted them back and up. From the very top, Beth could see across the fairgrounds to the racetrack. She thought about the race the next day and how much she wished she were riding Charmin'. Out they swung, and her stomach seemed to drop with the descent. Over and over they rode to the top, held their breaths, squealed, and dropped downward. The wheel went faster and faster, and Beth began to feel a little dizzy. "Aren't they giving us a long ride?" she asked.

"I think they keep it running until they have a line waiting," Dave said. "Are you getting tired of it?"

"No. I love it. Haven't been on one of these since I was little."

They were almost on top again. Clammy leaned over the side and called down to them. "How you doing?"

"Okay," Dave answered. "You?"

Clammy made a face and gripped the bar in front of him as his seat swung out and down.

It was another five minutes before the attendants started to unload the Ferris wheel. Since they had been last on, they were now last off. Dave held Beth's hand as she jumped down from the seat. It was a good thing. Her balance was off from the motion of the ride, and she staggered into him. He put an arm out to steady her.

"I think I'm going to be sick," Clammy said.

They looked at Clammy. His face was gray.

"There's a john in the exhibition hall," Dave said.

Clammy clamped his hands over his mouth and ran off.

"He started feeling bad when we got to the top the first time," Zosh told them.

"Poor guy." Beth was sympathetic. "I got a little dizzy myself."

"I hope he's going to be okay." Zosh looked worried.

"Once he throws up, he'll be fine," Dave assured her. "It's just motion sickness."

They walked over to the exhibition hall and waited outside. When Clammy came out, he didn't look much better. "Shouldn't have eaten all that junk," he muttered.

He had eaten a lot of hot dogs. They had joked about the irresistible attraction the food stands presented to him.

On the way home, he sat slumped in the backseat, saying nothing. "I hope you feel better," Zosh said as they pulled into his driveway.

"Ayeh. I'm bound to. Couldn't feel much worse." He pushed the door open. "Be at your house by eleven-thirty," he said to Dave.

Beth could hardly get to sleep. She kept thinking about the race the next day. What lousy luck that Clammy had gotten sick tonight. She hoped he would get enough sleep. In the race, he'd need every bit of concentration he could muster. Charmin' just had to win.

She wanted to get to sleep so the next day would come faster. Even though she couldn't ride Charmin', it was exciting to be a part of it. Mr. Fuller had invited her to go with them to the fairgrounds to give Charmin' his last grooming. She'd be with them until the very last minute. He'd been really nice to her, especially considering she had come close to ruining the day for everyone.

If you said one word over and over, it was supposed to relax you. You had to visualize it in your mind. Dave, she thought, picturing the name in block letters. *Dave.* She wrote it mentally in script. DAVE, in capitals. Dave, in small letters. DAVE, as big as a billboard. Dave, scrawled in green paint. Dave, in red neon.

She was in the stable area at the fairground, but it was weird. Riverdale Junior High was right next door. "Hurry up and get the saddle," Mr. Fuller said. "There are only two minutes until the race." She ran frantically around the stable. She couldn't find the stable. She couldn't find the saddle anywhere. "Hurry up. Hurry up." Amy and Darlene were standing in the door. "You're going to miss the race." Where could she have put the saddle? She ran into one of the stalls. There was a saddle lying in the corner. She picked it up and hurried outside. "What ails you?" Mr. Fuller glared at the saddle. "You can't use that." She looked down. She was holding a big, black Western saddle, ornamented with silver disks. She could hear the bell ringing in the school. "You're going to be late," Mr. Fuller scolded.

"Beth?"

She opened her eyes. Her father was standing in the doorway. "I hate to wake you so early, honey, but Mr. Fuller's on the phone."

Beth struggled to wake up. Was she still dreaming?

"Honey? He says it's important. Something about the race."

She jumped out of bed, still disoriented. "Mr. Fuller?"

"Yes. On the phone."

She hurried downstairs. "Mornin', Beth," Mr. Fuller said when she answered. "Looks like we got ourselves a problem."

"What's wrong?"

"Can you beat it? Mizziz Ellis just called me. Clammy's turned up with the chicken pox."

The chicken pox! Only little kids got the chicken pox. This must be part of her crazy dream.

"Beth. You there?" Mr. Fuller asked.

"Yes. . . . The chicken pox." Beth thought she couldn't have heard right.

"Ayeh. He thought it was something he ate at the carnival, but his face blossomed out this mornin', and Mizziz Ellis called the doctor. Temperature's a hundred and three."

"That's terrible."

"Dave and I been having words about what to do. He wanted to withdraw the hoss, but I figured to give you a shot at it. What do you think?"

She couldn't believe it. Mr. Fuller was going to let her ride Charmin' in the race! "Oh, yes. Oh, yes, I want to. Oh, yes, you really think I can do it? Oh, wow!"

She looked at her dad, who had followed her into the kitchen, and grinned madly. He raised an eyebrow questioningly.

"You think your folks will let you?" Percy asked. "They might have some objections."

"They'll let me. My dad's standing right here. Hold on." She held the receiver against her chest. "Daddy!

Mr. Fuller wants me to ride Charmin' in the race today." She was beside herself with excitement. "You don't mind, right?"

"In the race! Beth . . ." he hesitated.

"What's wrong?"

"Racing's an entirely different issue from pleasure riding or even showing." He sounded concerned. "We're going to have to discuss this."

"I don't see what there is to discuss." She frowned and put the phone receiver back to her ear. "Can I call you right back, Mr. Fuller?"

"Ayeh. And, Beth, you might tell your folks there have been boys your age who've ridden in this race, and none of 'em got hurt. Don't see why a girl couldn't do it."

"Thanks, Mr. Fuller." He wasn't so dumb, she thought.

"We'd better get your mother in on this." Charles called to his wife, "Honey, you dressed? We need you."

"Clammy's sick. He's got chicken pox." Beth tried to keep her voice calm, rational. "Either I ride Charmin' or he doesn't get entered. If he doesn't get in the race, the Fullers lose out on the prize money, and they need it."

"Hold on, Beth. There are some gaps in your reasoning." Charles went on in a tone Beth knew only too well. "First, the Fullers know everyone in the county, and there must be someone else who could ride the horse. Second, there is no guarantee the horse will win, so your argument about the prize money is theoretical."

"It sounds as if you have Beth on trial." Elinor Bridgewater had come in on his speech. "What is all this?"

"Mr. Fuller's asked me to ride Charmin' in the race today, Mom. It's the biggest thing that ever happened to me. You understand. You've seen me ride him. Tell Dad I can do it."

"Oh, Beth." Elinor spoke softly, but looked very worried. "I know you ride well, but being in a race is a different story from you and Clammy racing alone on the track. Dad and I have been to races, and we've seen experienced jockeys knocked off their horses—I remember one in Florida who was badly injured!" She put her arm around Beth's shoulder, but Beth pulled away. "Oh, honey, don't look so unhappy."

"Anytime you get on a horse there's some danger." Beth kept her jaw tight, fighting back emotion. "And other kids my age have ridden in this race. Of course, they were *boys*. You've always said your girls could do anything men could do, but maybe you didn't mean it."

Charles shook his head, but he couldn't suppress a smile. "Okay. I'll do this much. I'll talk to Percy Fuller."

He put in the call. Beth watched anxiously as he talked. He seemed to be nodding a lot. That was a good sign.

"Well?" she asked when he hung up.

"He says you're an excellent rider—in fact, a natural. I didn't argue that, despite the fortune I've spent on lessons. The horse responds to you better than to anyone else. A lot of locals have ridden in the race. There have been no accidents." He turned to his wife. "Perhaps we're being a trifle overprotective?"

"But . . . she's our baby. . . ."

"Not exactly. No tantrums. No tears. No 'if you don't let me, I'll never speak to you again.' I think she can handle it."

Beth threw her arms around him. "Daddy, I love you!" She pulled back and kissed her mother on the cheek. "I'll be okay. I promise, Mom." She looked up at the clock. "Nine! I've got to go start grooming him!" she exclaimed.

"In your pajamas?" Elinor gave in. "Go put on some clothes. I'm going to fix you breakfast. You don't want to faint in the middle of the race, do you?"

Beth ran to her room and threw on a pair of shorts. She came down and grabbed a glass of juice her mother had poured and picked up an English muffin. "I can't eat more than this," she said. "I just couldn't get it down, okay?"

She was out the door to the shed before her mother could answer. "Charmin'," she called as she ran into the barn. She heard a soft whinny and smiled. She opened the door to his stall and gasped. She could see the figure of a man standing in the corner. He moved out of the shadows.

"Dave!"

"You startled me," he said.

"What are you doing in here?" she asked.

He didn't answer right away. Then he said, "Beth. I have to talk to you. You can't ride him in the race."

"C'mon," she said. "I've had about all I can take this morning. I feel like a yo-yo. Your father wants me to ride him. My father doesn't want me to. I want to. Dad says all right. You don't want me to."

"There's more at stake than just a horse race," Dave said. "I'm going to level with you."

"Yes?" Beth waited.

"I want to show you something." He took Charmin's bridle and led him over to the front of the box stall. Light shone through a dusty window higher up in the barn wall. Dave peered at Charmin's nose. "You can't see in here," he said. "We'll have to take him outside."

Beth pushed open the stall door, and Dave led Charmin' through the barn. "I'm in serious trouble if this horse races."

"What kind of trouble?" Something in his voice scared her.

"You'll see."

Beth rolled back the barn door and looked right into Percy Fuller's face.

"Thought I might find you here, Dave," he said.

"Are you following me?"

"Guess I am. Didn't like leavin' things between us the way they were."

Beth could feel the tension between the two men. Dave said nothing. He just looked at his father.

"You're keeping something from me, son." Percy's lined face looked worried. "You've been fightin' and arguin' and carryin' on 'bout racing this hoss. Dave, you never in your life turned and walked away when I was talking to you like you did this mornin'. All over racin' this hoss. Now, what is it about?"

He had been going to tell her something. Beth hoped he would tell them both. She felt sorry for Mr. Fuller and nervous for Dave.

Dave took a deep breath. There was silence. He stared down at the ground. "There's nothing to tell," he said finally. "I'm against horse racing on principle. We've been over all this before."

Dave was lying. It made Beth feel even worse.

"That's all you've got to say to me?" Percy asked. Dave nodded. "Here, Beth." Percy held out a green satin shirt. "Picked up the colors at Clammy's. You've got jodhpurs and boots, right?"

Beth held up the jockey shirt. She couldn't get excited because of Dave, but she wanted to cheer Mr. Fuller up. He looked as glum as she felt. "I think it's gorgeous," she said. "I'm going to feel like a real jockey."

"Better start." Mr. Fuller smiled at her. "You'll be on the track in a few hours." He held up a green saddle blanket. "Heah's Charmin's outfit. Get yourself dressed, and we'll move on over to the grounds."

Dave had wanted to show her something. Something about Charmin' that he wasn't going to show her in front of his father. How could she get rid of Mr. Fuller for a little while?

"You'll give me a hand cleaning tack, won't you, Dave?" Percy was obviously trying to make peace with his son, and Beth wasn't going to be able to see him alone. Would Dave give her some sign?

"I'll help you." He sounded defeated.

"If we win, half the prize money is yours. Half for the feed bills. Half for you," Percy said.

Now Beth knew she had to win the race. Whatever was bothering Dave couldn't be *that* serious. She had overreacted. If she won the race, his real troubles were over. He could go back to school.

CHAPTER 10

When they got to the fairgrounds, Beth weighed in, holding her saddle. Then she walked Charmin' around the track to limber him up. Mr. Fuller went to find programs. He came back holding mimeographed sheets listing the day's races and entries. Ten horses were running for the Pearson Prize. Mr. Fuller recognized all but four of the owners' names. Six were locals. All of their horses were listed as long shots. The odds on Charmin' were 60 to 1. The other four horses, imports from bigger tracks, all had more favorable odds. The longest shot of the "ringers" was 10 to 1 on a horse called Aristo. Beth recognized the owner's name: Joe Carl. That must be the Mr. Carl who had been so interested in Charmin'. The paddock area was busy. Jockeys, trainers, and owners milled around. Mr. Fuller knew some of them.

"Where's Clammy?" a big, red-faced man in overalls asked, looking at Beth in her silks.

"Got chicken pox, Jesse," Mr. Fuller explained.

"You goin' with a greenhorn?" the man asked.

"Beth heah's not exactly a greenhorn," Mr. Fuller answered. "She knows the hoss better'n anyone."

"Good. Good. Glad to heah it." The man smiled. "Little girl still looks wet behind the ears to me."

"Could be youah eyes are failin'," Mr. Fuller drawled. "Age certainly hasn't improved your manners. Don't pay him any mind," he added to Beth, who was glaring. "He'd like to get you riled up so his nag would have a chance. Maybe this year he'll do better than he did before. Isn't too hard to do better than last place."

"Hmmph." The man turned away.

"There's the guy who told Clammy he was interested in buying Charmin'." Beth pointed out Mr. Carl, who was coming out of the stable talking intently to his jockey. Behind him, Al led out a large gray horse. "And that must be Aristo."

"He's sure giving his jockey an earful," Mr. Fuller said. Mr. Carl and the jockey had walked to one side, away from other people.

"Look at the horse," Dave said. Aristo was dancing around. Al was holding the bridle in both hands and leaning into the horse to control him.

"Look at his eyes." Dave grabbed his father's arm. The horse's eyes were wild and rolling, as if he were frightened. "I'll bet my shirt he's been given uppers."

"Uppers?" Beth asked.

"Drugs to make him run faster," Dave said angrily.

"Does look a bit peculiar," Mr. Fuller agreed as the horse tried to rear back.

"What did I tell you about these races?" Dave urged. "It isn't too late to scratch Charmin'."

Mr. Carl had caught sight of Aristo's wildness. He and the jockey hurried over to Al. They saw him gesture at the stable. Al wheeled the horse around and took him back inside. Mr. Carl saw Beth and said something to the jockey, then they both walked over.

"Hello, young lady," he greeted her. "Where's your friend?"

"Sick," she answered.

"And you're riding." It was a statement, not a question. "Better be careful out there." He smiled as if he were joking. "Some of these boys are awful anxious to win. Good-looking horse, huh?" he said to the jockey. "He may be the one you have to beat."

The jockey had leathery skin and dark brown eyes. "We will," he said, smiling at Beth.

"You the owner?" Mr. Carl asked Mr. Fuller.

Mr. Fuller indicated Dave. "Belongs to my son."

"Got some things to take care of." The jockey looked at Mr. Carl.

"Right. Go ahead. Just wanted you to meet your competition. See you right before the race. About ten minutes, Eduardo." He dismissed him. "Where'd you pick up this colt, son?" he asked Dave.

"It's a long story," Dave answered.

"I'm a good listener," Mr. Carl said.

"Hey, Beth, your parents are here." Dave took the bridle from Beth's hand. "You'll have to excuse us," he said to Mr. Carl, leading Charmin' toward the Bridgewaters, who were standing at the paddock fence.

"I might be interested in buying your horse." Mr. Carl took a step after him. "Just like to know a little about his background."

"He's not for sale," Mr. Fuller said.

Beth's parents were very excited, and so was Zosh. The odds, chalked up on a blackboard, were staying at 60 to 1. Zosh had asked Charles to bet $2 for her and stood to win $120 if Charmin' came in first.

"Just be careful," Elinor cautioned her daughter.

"Relax, hon," Charles Bridgewater reassured her. "Beth can handle herself. Go out there and win, sweetheart."

"I have a real feeling you're going to." Zosh's face was pink with excitement. "And my feelings are usually right."

"Great, Zosh." Beth laughed. "Between your feelings and Charmin's speed, I won't have to do anything."

Percy Fuller came up next to Beth at the paddock fence. "You stand right over there," he told the Bridgewaters, pointing in front of the bleachers, and Beth could see what looked like a high wire across the track. "That's the finish line, as you prob'ly know. You'll have the best view."

"Good luck, sweetheart." Charles leaned over and kissed her, and then her mother gave her a hug and kiss. Charles took Elinor by one hand and Zosh by the other. "We'd better get places."

"Now, you're in fourth position," Percy explained after her parents left. "That should be a good spot. The way this hoss runs, I wouldn't hold him back at all. Go for the front and stay there, okay?"

Beth nodded. It was the only strategy she knew.

"And watch out for that jockey Eduardo." Dave was frowning. "If they did drug the horse, they wouldn't be above other sleazy tricks. Keep away from him."

"She's got to start out next to him. His hoss has the third post position. Just show him your dust, Beth."

"I'll do my best."

Mr. Fuller gave her a hand and lifted her into the saddle. "Time to go. Good luck, Beth." He squeezed her arm, and Beth, whose spirits were already high, felt any more excitement might be unbearable. Mr. Fuller took the bridle and led her out to the oval.

She heard her father's voice calling encouragement as they walked past the small bleachers. She caught sight of him standing against the fence, and grinned. Charmin' pranced as if to salute his fans.

Then they were at the gate. Her heart was banging against her chest. Charmin' went in easily. Beneath her, Beth sensed energy waiting to uncoil. Her body tensed. Her hands trembled. There was the clang of a bell. The bar dropped in front of them. They were off.

As they bounced forward out of the gate, Beth saw something black crack in front of her face. Charmin' faltered. Could it really have happened? The jockey on her right had hit Charmin' with his whip. Eduardo! The gray horse brushed against her, forcing her aside. As she moved, a bay on her left shot forward. Charmin' was unsteady, boggled. Beth cried out softly as they dropped back. Now there was a solid wall of horses ahead of them and no room to move up. As they came around the far turn, Aristo was well in the lead. Behind him and blocking access to the inside were the bay and a black horse. Beth felt angry and desperate.

"IT'S ARISTO IN THE LEAD BY THREE LENGTHS," the loudspeaker boomed. "ECLIPSE IS IN SECOND, AND A NECK BEHIND IS WHIRLWIND."

They were making for the clubhouse turn. Charmin' was steadier now, anxious to race, but no hole to break through. Beth had no alternative. She would have to move to the outside, costing her precious distance.

"AS THEY ROUND THE TURN, IT'S STILL ARISTO, HOLDING ON TO HIS THREE-LENGTH LEAD. WHIRLWIND HAS MOVED INTO SECOND, AND MAKING A MOVE NOW IS MOLLY'S FOLLY."

"We have to do it, Charmin'. We have to," Beth coaxed him. Now they were on the outside. "Show them, Charmin', the dirty, lousy rats. We'll show them."

"AS THEY COME INTO THE STRETCH, IT'S ARISTO IN FIRST. MOLLY'S FOLLY IS IN SECOND AND CHALLENGING. WHIRLWIND HAS DROPPED BACK TO THIRD. THE NUMBER-FOUR HORSE HAS GONE WIDE ON THE OUTSIDE. HE'S MAKING A MOVE. FROM EIGHTH PLACE!"

Charmin' surged forward. They were flying. The other horses seemed almost to be standing still. "CHARMIN', THE NUMBER-FOUR HORSE, IS IN FOURTH PLACE AND MAKING A STRONG BID."

They were neck and neck with the black horse. Beth had the whip in her hand. Should she use it? They were past the black and closing on second place.

"CHARMIN' IS POURING IT ON. A SIXTY-TO-ONE HORSE! WHAT A HORSE RACE!"

The finish line looked close. "Go, Charmin', go!" His hooves pounded. They were passing the gray. She saw a startled look on Eduardo's face.

"HE DID IT!" the announcer screamed. "IT'S CHARMIN' BY A LENGTH. A LOCAL HORSE HAS WON THE PEARSON PRIZE!"

Beth could hear the cheering. People were screaming and applauding. She tried to look back and find her parents, but she was way past the finish line, and Charmin' was still running flat out. "You won!" She didn't know if she was laughing or crying. "You won, Charmin'!"

She pulled back harder on the reins and finally slowed him down. They were almost halfway around the track again. She turned and came back at a slow canter. The cheering got louder. Dave and Mr. Fuller were standing in the middle of the track in front of the stadium. Percy held out his hand and took hold of Charmin's bridle.

"This is the big moment!" Mr. Fuller cheered, leading the horse to the winner's circle. "Danged fine riding." He reached back and patted Beth.

Beth couldn't stop grinning. It was the happiest moment of her life.

"Can't we just split?" Dave muttered. "I don't want any pictures."

"What in the world ails you, son? Grumbling and complaining. You'd think we lost the race." Mr. Fuller was smiling broadly.

A man dressed in a white suit placed a wreath of carnations around Charmin's neck. Beth looked up to see her father taking a picture as the man handed Mr. Fuller a check and a trophy.

Mr. Fuller turned and gave it to Dave.

A photographer ran up and knelt just outside the winner's circle. Dave grabbed the bridle and swung Charmin' around. Beth slipped to the side.

"Hey, wait," the photographer yelled as Dave trotted Charmin' and Beth back to the barn.

Zosh ran toward them, waving a fistful of money. "I'm rich!" she called.

"Let's get him loaded fast." Dave pulled on Beth's arm, sliding her out of the saddle. He jerked at the girth. "Open the trailer," he ordered.

Beth felt cheated. She wasn't going to get to enjoy her victory. She jerked the back door open and looked at Dave. "I'd hoped you'd be happy," she said.

Mr. Fuller came up with her parents. He was still beaming. "They boxed you in in good shape, but you outsmarted them."

"I never thought you'd make it when you had to go so wide," her father said. "I think we've got one dandy rider in the family."

"I didn't think I'd make it, but I was so mad I would have tried anything."

"Well, there's tricks in every trade," Mr. Fuller said.

"If they coulda taken advantage of your inexperience, guess you can't rightly blame 'em."

"*Dirty* tricks. That Eduardo hit Charmin' with his whip as we came out of the gate. Didn't you see him?"

"No. And neither did the stewards, or they'd have disqualified him." Mr. Fuller frowned. "We could lodge a complaint and try to get his hoss thrown out of second place—"

"Why, Dad?" Dave asked quickly. "It would be Beth's word against his. We won the race. Now let's just go."

"It's a matter of fair play, Dave."

"How are you going to prove it? You don't stand a chance. Besides, you don't want to involve Beth in that sort of mess, do you?"

"Well . . . could be you're right. . . ." Mr. Fuller did not sound convinced.

"Let's get out of here, huh?" Dave moved to the driver's side of the van.

"Look!" Beth pointed at Mr. Carl and Eduardo, who were arguing in front of the stable. Eduardo was looking down at the ground.

"I think I'll just have a word with those two," Mr. Fuller said.

"Dad . . ." Dave reached out to stop him, but his father brushed his hand aside and strode over to the others.

"He doesn't know what he's doing!" Dave slammed into the van. He put it in gear and roared off.

Beth stood there, stunned.

Her mother moved over and stroked her hair, but said nothing.

"I guess Percy's telling that guy a thing or two," her father said. Percy was pointing and gesturing at Eduardo. Mr. Carl was shaking his head. They moved away from the jockey and walked over to the group.

"Looks like an apology is in order," Mr. Carl said to Beth. "I hear Eduardo might have accidentally hit your horse. He didn't even realize it."

"Accidentally?" Beth hadn't meant the word to come out so loudly.

"Of course. *If* he hit him, it was an accident. You and that horse cost me and some other people a lot of money today. Where'd you say you picked him up?" he asked Mr. Fuller.

"Didn't," was Mr. Fuller's only reply.

"Funny, but there's something very familiar about that animal. I might just have to make it my business to find out what." He smiled, but there was the hint of a threat under his seemingly light tone.

"Don't know what you're talking about, and I suspect you don't either." Mr. Fuller, hands on hips, looked down at the shorter man.

"We'll see."

Mr. Fuller turned away. "You folks mind giving me a lift home? There's some kind of a smell around here, and it ain't just from the hosses."

CHAPTER

11

The cicadas were singing constantly. That meant summer was really over. Beth had been so up for the race, and now she was experiencing a real letdown. Dave had not come near the farm since. Clammy would be "outa commission" for a week, if not more. Her mother had started packing boxes to get ready to go home. Beth hated the sight of them. The thought of leaving the farm . . . of leaving Charmin' . . . she couldn't let herself think about it. Couldn't waste her last days feeling sad. At least she could be useful—keep her promise to Zosh.

"It's time you learned to ride," she said to her one afternoon. "You've gotten comfortable around Dolly now, and it won't be like the first time, I promise."

"Oh, Beth, I don't know. I like her, but I don't know if I'm ready to ride her."

"Come on. I won't let you chicken out on me. I borrowed a lead from the Fullers. I'll be controlling the horse the whole time."

Beth saddled Dolly and demonstrated mounting several times. Finally Zosh agreed to try it and managed to swing her leg over the saddle. "See how easily you did that?" Beth congratulated her. "Here." She arranged Zosh's fingers. "Hold the reins like this. Now grip with the upper part of your legs. You feel secure?"

"Uh-uh." Zosh's blue eyes were wide.

Beth laughed. "Just relax. I'm going to lead you out to the meadow. We'll just walk for a while."

It was a long training lead, and once in the field Beth kept Dolly walking in wide circles around her. When Zosh looked more comfortable, Beth told her she was going to have Dolly do a slow trot.

"I'm going to fall off!" Zosh, who was bouncing up and down, grabbed hold of the saddle.

"No you're not. Now, just do what I say," Beth directed. "Stand up in the stirrups, then sit down. It's called posting."

"I can't. I have to hang on."

"No you don't. When you get the rhythm, it's easy. I'll call it out for you. Up . . . down. Up . . . down. Up . . . down." Beth couldn't help laughing. Zosh looked so intense. She missed the beat and bounced again. "Come on, Zosh," Beth encouraged. "Up . . . down. Keep those heels down. That's better. Up . . . down."

After they had made a few circles, Beth stopped counting out the rhythm, and although Zosh lost the beat occasionally, she managed to recover it. "Are you ready to try a canter yet?" Beth asked.

"No. No. No. Not a canter. Not today. I like walking best." Zosh laughed at herself.

"Okay." Beth stopped Dolly. "Tell you what, then. I'll take you off the lead, and you can walk her back to the barn yourself."

"But I don't know how to steer her," Zosh protested.

"You use the reins and your knees." Beth explained the techniques.

Zosh managed to get Dolly back to the barn, and once the lesson was completed, she was pleased with herself. She helped Beth brush the horse and volunteered to lead her out to the pasture.

They walked out to the lane, and Beth was startled to see her mother and two men, one with a huge camera and other equipment strapped to his back.

"Beth," her mother said excitedly, "these gentlemen are from the *Boston Globe.* They want pictures of you and Charmin'! This is James Allen. Mr. Allen is a sportswriter. And this is Bernie Moskowitz, a photographer for the paper."

The men shook hands with Zosh and Beth. "If the timing at the fair was accurate, you got a real wonder horse here. We think this could be a major story," James Allen said.

"You'd better give me a nice smile." Bernie Moskowitz raised his camera. "Your picture is liable to be all over the country."

"You're kidding!" Beth was thrilled. "Even in Riverdale, Connecticut?"

"Most people in the suburbs read *The New York Times*. There's a good chance they'll pick it up," Allen told her. "It's got all the ingredients: an unseasoned horse, a girl who's never raced, and a time that would look good in the Belmont. Good thing I do my homework. Picked up a little article in the *Manchester Star*."

"What'd you wear in the race?" Bernie Moskowitz asked.

"Green silks," Beth answered. "Percy Fuller let me keep them."

"Put 'em on, will you? I want some pictures of you and the wonder horse."

"Come on, Zosh." Beth put her arm around her friend. "You brush Charmin' while I change, okay?"

"Sure." Zosh beamed.

"Let's get some info first," Allen said. "How old are you, Beth?"

She hesitated. If she told him, and it was in the paper, Dave would find out she was only—

"Beth's fifteen," her mother said proudly, "and wait until you see her handle that big horse."

"Do you have to put my age in?" Beth gave her mother a dirty look.

"Adds to the human interest," Allen answered. "Okay, Beth, now start at the beginning. Tell me everything you can about the horse and your involvement with him."

It was a story Beth loved to tell. Allen took a lot of

notes, asked a lot of questions. When he was finished, Beth changed into her silks.

"Beth," Elinor said, "don't you think you should call Dave? He really should be here, too. After all, he owns Charmin'!"

"That Dave Fuller you're talking about?" Allen asked. "We've been trying to get hold of him, but he hasn't returned our calls. Stopped by there first, as a matter of fact, and his father directed us up here."

"I'll go see if he's in," Elinor Bridgewater said.

Beth cantered Charmin' up and down the lane, showing him off for them. Moskowitz took a lot of pictures. They had just finished and Beth was signing a release when Dave came running around the barn. She went to meet him. "Isn't this neat! These guys are from the *Boston Globe*!"

Dave ignored her. He rushed right past her, leaving her standing there feeling ridiculous.

"What do you think you're doing!" he yelled at the reporters. "No one gave you permission to come up here and take pictures. Just hand over the film!"

"Hey now, hold on, young fellow," Allen said quietly. "What are you getting so exercised about? We're covering a story. This horse is big news, and the publicity is sure not going to hurt you or the horse."

"You don't know anything about it," Dave said. "He's my horse, and you can't use his picture without my permission. And I'm not giving it, see?"

Allen looked at Elinor. "You live here?"

She nodded.

"You give us permission to come on this property and take pictures?"

"Yes, I did." Elinor looked at Dave. "I don't see the harm."

"Beth," Allen said clearly, "did you sign a release?"

"Yes." Beth looked at Dave. "I'm sorry. I didn't know you—"

He started to say something, then turned his back on her. "I own the horse," he insisted to Allen, "and I say no pictures!" He lunged suddenly at Bernie Moskowitz. "I want the film!"

Allen caught him by the left arm, deflecting him from the photographer. Dave turned around and raised his right hand as if to strike the reporter.

"No!" Elinor rushed over. "No fighting!" She caught his upraised arm. "Please, Dave!"

"Cool it, kid," Bernie Moskowitz said. "You don't want to be up on assault charges, do you?"

Without another word, Dave pulled away, turned, and, back rigid, ears red, stalked off around the barn.

"Well, what do you make of that?" Elinor looked stunned.

"The kid some kind of psycho?" Moskowitz asked.

"No! He is not!" Beth said angrily.

"He's usually a very nice, polite boy." Elinor shrugged. "I just don't know what got into him."

"You'd think he'd want all the P.R. he could get," Allen said. "Doesn't make sense."

"Well, it does to him!" Beth couldn't bear their standing around talking about Dave as if he were crazy. "So why don't you just knock it off!" She could feel the tears threatening and ran for the house. She rushed upstairs to her room and threw herself on the bed. She felt awful. She hadn't meant to do anything wrong—but somehow she had. Now he was gone. She was leaving soon, and she'd probably never see him again.

The next day Zosh did her best to cheer Beth up. They went on a wildflower walk in the morning and made daisy chains just as if they were little kids. They found hyacinth-blue chicory and wove wreaths for their hair. Zosh was good to be with. She seemed able to fit right in with Beth's mood. She was able to be quiet and listen, but she could join in with silly stuff, too, and clowned around with the flowers.

Beth's dad was standing outside the house as they came up from the meadow. He was waving a paper at them. "Come here, Miss Celebrity," he called.

"Beth, it must be the article!" Zosh started jogging up the hill. "I can't wait to see!"

Beth couldn't wait either, and she pushed back thoughts of Dave and the way he had acted.

"Look!" Her dad held out the *Boston Globe.* "Almost a whole page in the sports section!"

There was an enormous picture of Beth on Charmin' taken from a side view. Charmin's head and ears were up, and he was looking right at the camera.

"Isn't he gorgeous!" Beth grinned.

"His rider isn't exactly chopped liver." Charles Bridgewater gave her a hug.

"I like that one of you, Beth." Zosh pointed. In another shot, the photographer had caught them in mid-canter, and they looked as if they had floated off the ground.

"They're great!" Beth was tickled.

She was reading the story. It did sound like a fairy tale . . . now, almost like a dream . . . like she was reading about someone else.

"I'm going to have to run down to the store and buy them out," her father said. "Sarah Wentworth dropped this one off, but I want a gross at least."

"Hey, star." Her mother was standing in the doorway smiling happily. "You have a fan on the phone."

"Who?" Beth didn't get many phone calls in New Hampshire.

"Dave. I guess he's over his mad. He apologized for his behavior yesterday. I imagine he's seen the paper and realizes he acted rather badly. . . ."

Beth did not wait to hear any more. She shoved the paper at Zosh and ran into the house.

"Beth?" It *was* Dave.

"Hi," she said.

"There's a chicken pot pie supper at the Grange tonight," Dave said. "My mother thought you folks might want to go."

She was taken by surprise. She had assumed he'd called about the newspaper. "A supper?"

"Yeah. It's put on by the Rebekahs. Ma belongs, and I can vouch for the chow.'

Was he just calling because his mother had told him to? And had he seen the paper? She was afraid to ask.

"I don't know," she said. "I'll have to ask my parents."

"I really hope you'll come," he said. "You could talk them into it."

He sounded really anxious. "Okay," she said. "Mom and Dad will probably want to."

"Good. Be there by seven. I'll be looking for you."

She just couldn't figure him out, she thought as she hung up the phone. Yesterday he'd been rude to her in front of all those people; today he'd just about insisted she come to the supper.

It took no convincing to get her parents to agree. They were really good to her, she thought. They almost always tried to make her happy. She gave her mother a squeeze and saw a glad look come over her face. "I haven't always been the greatest, Mom," she whispered. Before her mother could answer, she turned to Zosh. "Come on," she said. "We have to pick out what we're going to wear."

She fussed with her hair. "I don't want to wear a ponytail or braids," she confided to Zosh. "I don't want to look like a kid."

"You could wear it loose," Zosh suggested. "It's so long, it looks really pretty."

"It's too hot. I need it off my face."

"Can I try something with it? If you don't like it, you can always change it."

"Sure," Beth agreed. Zosh made thin braids on either side of the front, then tied them together with a ribbon in back. The long dark hair hung freely over Beth's shoulders.

"I like it," Beth declared. "Come on. Let's get dressed."

She put on her blue sundress, not unaware that it made her eyes look bluer and showed off her tan.

Zosh had bought a very simple white sundress with some of the money she had won betting on Charmin'. She wore it now for the first time, and Beth was amazed. Living with Zosh every day, she had adjusted to the gradual weight loss without really noticing it. Now, with Zosh in the new dress, it was apparent. Her hair had streaked blond-white in the sun, and she had tanned a warm, golden color.

"What a couple of knockouts," Charles Bridgewater said when they came downstairs, ready to go.

"Our baby's growing up!" Elinor said.

"Mo-ther!" Beth hated it when her mother referred to her as "her baby."

"I think she already has." Her father smiled at Beth. "And not just physically."

"Zosh, you look beautiful." Elinor took Zosh's shoulders and turned her around. "That dress suits you perfectly."

"Both of our girls have certainly blossomed. It must be the country air," Charles said.

"It's been a wonderful summer." Zosh beamed. "I don't know how to tell you—" She stopped, blushing. "I . . . I don't think I've ever said . . . thank you."

"We're all glad you came. Right, Beth?" Elinor turned to her daughter.

Beth made a face at her that meant, Don't put me on. "Zosh doesn't have to be told," she said. "She knows."

"We should be going somewhere fancier than a church supper," Charles said. "How about driving over to Manchester and hitting the Homestead Inn. I hear it's very good."

"No," Beth answered immediately. "I'd rather go to the supper."

"Aha!" Her father teased. "Is there something here that doesn't meet the eye? Or do you have your eye on someone?"

"Daddy, quit it!" Beth turned red. "We can go to dumb restaurants at home. How often do we get to go to a pot pie supper?"

" 'Methinks the lady doth protest too much,' " Charles said, quoting Shakespeare. "You can't fool your old dad. You didn't dress up to impress the chicken."

"I'll put my jeans back on if it'll make you happy." Beth started for the stairs. If her father could figure her out so easily, couldn't Dave?

"No, no, honey." Charles intercepted his daughter and gave her a hug. "I'm thrilled to see that you actually have legs. Now, come on, let's get going," he coaxed.

The supper was held in the Grange. Beth was relieved to see that most of the girls their age were in dresses. She looked around for Dave. Percy and Jack Fuller were standing in line waiting to be served, and Percy waved them over.

"Mighty nice write-up," he said. "Want to have supper with my favorite jockey. You line up to get your eats," he told them. "Then go outside to the lawn. They've got picnic tables set up. We'll save you places."

Beth wanted to ask about Dave but was too embarrassed. Zosh seemed to read her mind. "Where's Mrs. Fuller and Dave?" Zosh asked.

"Mother's helping to serve," Percy explained. "Dave brought her down heah in the Jeep, and I haven't seen him since. He'll be along soon, I figure."

The supper was delicious, as Dave had promised. The pies had homemade biscuit crusts and were filled with chicken and vegetables. There was corn on the cob and fresh dairy butter, salads loaded with garden greens and herbs, luscious purple-red tomatoes, and baked acorn squash.

After they had finished eating, they lined up for desserts.

"It looks good," Beth said to Zosh as they waited for their turn, "but I really don't feel hungry."

"It's funny Dave never showed up." Zosh was sympathetic.

"Yeah. He said seven o'clock." Beth looked at the

watch on her wrist. "It's almost eight. I guess he's not coming."

"Maybe he still will," Zosh said, trying to be encouraging.

"I doubt it. Why should he? He doesn't like me or anything." Beth said it, but she really hoped she was wrong.

"Yes he does. I can tell."

"How? How can you tell?" Beth was eager for any scrap of reassurance.

"Well, you haven't seen him with another girl, have you?"

"That doesn't mean anything. He probably has a girl in Virginia."

"Not the way he looks at you he doesn't." Zosh was emphatic.

"Well, he might look, but that's all he does." Beth giggled, cheered somehow by Zosh's words.

Beth took a big slab of peach pie. Sophie had a tiny sliver of chocolate cake.

"A month ago I would have had a little bit of everything," Zosh confessed as they made their way back to the table. "Look, Beth." She nudged her. Dave was standing next to his father, talking.

He looked great. He was wearing a blue-and-white-checked shirt and white jeans.

"You 'bout missed the supper," Percy was saying. "Better go see if there's anything left."

Dave went inside and came back with a plate full of

chicken pie. Where was he going to sit, Beth wondered. There was more room on the bench by his father and Jack.

"Am I crowding you?" Dave asked, sliding in on the bench next to her.

"Oh, no." Beth moved closer to Zosh to give him room. He put his plate down and shifted on the bench. Their legs touched.

Beth pushed the peach pie away. She couldn't eat a bite.

The grown-ups chatted over their coffee and dessert, mostly about the story in the paper. Dave was quiet, and Beth couldn't think of a thing to say. She could have kicked herself. The evening was going by, and she was sitting like a dummy.

Dave pushed his plate away. "The new Woody Allen movie is playing in Manchester. There's a nine o'clock show. Want to go?"

This was it. A real date. He had actually asked her for a real date. Her heart was beating so hard, she was afraid everyone could see it through her dress. "Sure," she said.

"Anybody else up for a movie?" Dave asked. Beth felt her body slump as she let out the breath she didn't even know she was holding.

The Fullers refused, and so did Zosh at first, but when the Bridgewaters said they would go, she changed her mind. Beth could have killed her dumb parents. She had really wanted to be alone with Dave.

"How about riding with me?" Dave asked Beth as they went out to the cars.

"Okay," she said. It probably didn't mean anything, she thought. He just didn't want to drive thirty miles by himself. She wasn't going to get her hopes up again.

"It's kind of a high step." He opened the Jeep door for her and took her arm as she climbed in.

"I was hoping no one else would come," he said as they were driving to Manchester. "But I thought your mother might think it was funny if I didn't ask."

"Why would she?" Beth could hardly believe it. He might just as well have said he wanted to be alone with her, too. "I go out at home, you know." So what if it had only been once, and with that jerk Paul Parsons. He'd held her hand in the movie until they both got all sweaty, and Beth, embarrassed, had pulled her hand away. She remembered sitting there, miserable, hands clasped together, and Paul tugging, trying to get her hand back until she'd finally given him a good whack with her elbow and told him to bug off. It made her cringe just to think about it. What if Dave held her hand? She started to get nervous, then realized he had said something. She hadn't been paying attention.

"I'm sorry? What did you say?" she asked.

"Just that I didn't want your mother to think I was robbing the cradle," Dave answered.

"Come off it." Beth was annoyed, especially since she could feel herself blushing. "I'm not exactly a baby, you know."

"Don't get mad." Dave reached over and patted her hand. "I didn't say you were. I guess I just wonder what I'm doing running after a sixteen-year-old."

Running after a sixteen-year-old! Those words lodged in Beth's mind, practically an admission that he *did* like her. It was a good thing the paper had only called her a young teenager.

After that, Beth hardly saw the movie, as she went over the slight conversation again and again in her mind. She had wondered if he would hold her hand or touch her in the darkness of the theater, but her parents and Zosh sat directly behind them. She didn't know if she was relieved or sorry, remembering the awful time with Paul.

"How'd you like it?" she asked him on the ride home.

"So-so," was all he said. He seemed silent, preoccupied.

"Wasn't Woody Allen funny?" Beth offered.

"Hm?"

"I thought Woody Allen was neat," she repeated.

"Typical Allen."

She tried a few more times. Finally he said, "Sorry, hon, I was thinking of something else."

"Hon"! Had he meant the word of endearment, or had it just slipped out, a thoughtless, meaningless term? And what had he been thinking about—could it have been her? Had he decided he was going to kiss her tonight?

They pulled into her driveway. Her parents' car was

not yet there. Dave turned off the motor and turned toward her. He leaned over and took her arms in his hands so she was facing him. She felt scared, but tingly.

"Do me a favor." He looked into her eyes; his brown ones were intense and serious.

"Yes." The word came out in a whisper.

"Don't give any more newspaper interviews."

Beth jerked away from him, hurt. She felt like a fool. Dave hadn't been thinking about her at all.

CHAPTER 12 "Today I think you ought to try and solo," Beth told Zosh the next morning. "Charmin' should be all right for an easy ride, and you can follow me on Dolly."

"But I haven't even cantered yet." Zosh looked uneasy.

"That's all right. We'll stay in the meadow and just walk and trot. Afterward I'll put you on the lead, and you can try a canter."

"I don't think I'm ready," Zosh protested.

Beth brushed aside her objections. "You didn't think you were ready yesterday and look how well you did. You're going to love it once you get used to it. Then we can take trail rides and stuff together."

"That would be fun." The idea obviously appealed to Zosh. "I just wish I weren't scared."

"You'll get over it. Anyone with brains is scared at first," Beth reassured her. "Come on, help me get Charmin' and Dolly in the barn to feed them. We can't ride for a while after that."

"That's all right with me," Zosh said, and they both laughed.

They walked into the barn. A rope with a round board attached at the bottom hung from the beam in the clear center section of the barn. Someone had put it there for swinging, and Beth hardly ever passed it by. She grabbed it as high as she could reach, ran as far as she could, and then leaped on to swing back in a long arc. The morning was alive with happiness and possibilities. The night before might have been disappointing in some ways, but there had been much more good than bad. She'd had a date with Dave; he'd called her "hon"; and he'd talked about running after her. That was enough to make her airborne.

Sophie was at the grain bin. "Six scoops for Charmin' and four for Dolly, right?" she asked.

"Yeah." Beth jumped down. "I'll go let them in." She started for the back door. "Hey, Charmin'," she called. "Chow time."

She was not greeted by Charmin's usual knock. He must be grazing in the pasture, she thought. Dolly was waiting when she opened the door, but Charmin' was nowhere to be seen. She led the little mare into her stall. "That's funny," she said to Zosh. "They usually stay together. I'll have to go look for him."

Beth jogged up the lane, calling the horse's name.

She got to the top of the rise and looked down into the little pasture and the larger one beyond. She couldn't see him anywhere. This had never happened before. Uneasy, she started back to the barn to tell Zosh she would have to go farther to find him, then stopped, aghast. The bars to the lane were down. She must have forgotten to put them up when she put Charmin' back in yesterday. How could she have been so stupid!

"He's gotten out!" she yelled as she ran into the barn. "It's all my fault. I left the bars down yesterday, and he's gone!"

"Oh, Beth." Zosh's eyes were wide. "What are you going to do?"

"We've got to find him. What would Dave think? I could shoot myself!"

"I'll help you. Do you have any idea where to start?" Zosh asked.

"I've got to stay calm and think." Beth was anything but calm, pulling at her ponytail and biting her lip.

"Why don't I go up the road and you go down?" Zosh suggested.

"But he could be anywhere. He could have crossed the road. He could have gone off through the back woods." The possibilities were endless. "Let's go talk to my dad. He's usually good in a crisis." Beth had started running for the house before the words were out of her mouth.

Charles Bridgewater tried his best to soothe his

daughter. "He's just not going to go far," he reasoned. "Why would he?"

"Why wouldn't he?" Beth answered. "I left the bars down, and he's free. It's like he's out of jail."

"Horses don't reason like people, no matter how smart you think Charmin' is," Charles said. "Look," he suggested, "let's jump in the car and cover these back roads. If he's grazing in a field, we'll see him. We can also stop and alert the neighbors, okay?"

It made sense for them not to go running wild in different directions, Beth had to agree. She even started to feel a little hopeful. When the morning had passed with no sign or word of Charmin', however, she began to feel desperate.

"We'd better go home and call the Fullers," her father said.

Beth couldn't bear to do that. "Let me look some more," she begged. "I've just got to find him before Dave hears about it."

"You know, he still could be in the pasture," Zosh said. "Just because the bars are down doesn't mean he *had* to go out."

"That's true ... and I didn't really look there very well." Beth clung to the idea.

"Maybe he got hungry and we'll find him at the barn."

Beth prayed she was right.

Elinor Bridgewater was standing on the porch when they drove in.

"Is Charmin' here?" Beth bolted out of the car, waiting for her mother to say yes.

Elinor shook her head. "You didn't find him?" she asked.

"No." Beth started to cry.

"Don't cry, honey." Her father put his arms around her. "He'll turn up, honest."

"Why don't we look in the pastures," Zosh said. "There are trees and groves. He could easily be there."

"Go ahead, sweetheart," Charles said. "Then if he isn't there, we'll call the Fullers, and organize a big search. I'll stay here by the phone in case he's spotted by a neighbor. Okay?"

"All right." Please let him be in the pasture, she thought. Please. "Let's take Dolly. We can take turns riding her."

"That's all right. You ride. I'd really rather walk," Zosh said. She made an exaggerated, scared face, trying to cheer Beth up.

The girls went down the lane to the small pasture, and through the open gate to the much larger one. Beth kept calling Charmin's name, feeling more discouraged each time. They got to the brook that formed a boundary, and made their way to the pine grove. It was one of Beth's favorite spots. She thought of it as her temple in the woods, but today it held no comfort for her.

"Beth, come here!" Zosh called. "Quick!"

Zosh was standing by the split-rail fence that divided the farm from Sarah Wentworth's property. A top rail had been knocked down, and a horse could easily have gotten across.

"Maybe Charmin' got out here instead of up by the barn." Zosh pointed to the damaged fence.

"You're right!" Even little Dolly stepped over the remaining rail with no problem. There were woods on the other side, but an old overgrown logging road made an easy trail to follow.

If they turned left, they would probably come out on Pumpkin Hill Road, near Sarah Wentworth's. "Let's try this way first." Beth pointed to the right where the old road went deeper into the woods.

They had gone perhaps a quarter mile when Dolly suddenly stopped and pricked up her ears. "She hears something. Shhh," Beth cautioned Zosh. "What do you hear, girl? What is it, Dolly?"

As if in answer, Dolly gave a low whinny. Then she whinnied again, louder this time.

Beth leaned down in the saddle and whispered urgently, "Who is it, babe?"

There was an answering whinny!

"Charmin'!" Beth and Zosh both yelled. It was coming from the trail ahead. Zosh started running toward the sound, and Dolly, without urging, broke into a trot. There was a rutted path to the right, and the mare stopped, her head up, listening. She whinnied again, and again was answered.

"It *is* Charmin'." Beth could hardly believe her luck. "Run, Zosh," she said as she turned Dolly down the path and cantered off. A few hundred yards ahead of them were the remains of an old building. As she came up to it, Beth saw it was an abandoned shed. Excited whinnies were coming from inside. Beth jumped off Dolly, dropping the reins to the ground, and peered through an old window. It was dirty, broken in one corner, and covered with cobwebs. "I can see him," she hollered to Zosh. "Charmin's in here!" She ran around to the door at the front of the shed. A hinge dangled from the top on one side. A padlock was secured on the latch. She started pulling frantically at it, trying to pry the door free from the other rusty hinge.

Zosh came up panting and out of breath.

"Help me, Zosh," she said. "Someone's locked Charmin' in the shed."

Breathing hard and sweating, Zosh wedged her fingers in next to Beth's and they pulled as hard as they could. They could get the crack to widen to about six inches, but the hinge held fast.

"What are we going to do?" Zosh said as they tugged and strained.

"We've got to get him out!" Beth felt desperate. That was all she could think.

"It's not coming loose," Zosh said. "It's not even moving."

"We need something to pry it with." Beth let go and ran into the woods looking for a stick. She found a small limb on the ground and ran back to Zosh. "Pull," she said, "while I wedge this in." She got the stick between the door and the wall, and they both pushed on it, trying to use it as a lever. The stick snapped.

"We'd better get help," Zosh said. "We'd better get your father."

"No," Beth thought quickly. "Go to Mrs. Wentworth's. It's closer than the farm. Call the police. I'll stay here with Charmin'."

"How far is it?" Zosh was sweating from the run through the woods.

"At least a mile. Probably more. I know this is going to scare you, but you're just going to have to ride Dolly. You're tired, and on foot it will take you forever."

Zosh looked scared. "But I can't ride well enough. Why don't we both go?"

"Someone's trying to steal Charmin'," Beth said. "I'll bet it's that creepy Mr. Carl. Remember, he tried to get Dave to sell him? I've got to stay here in case he comes. I can't leave Charmin'."

"But what if I fall off?" Zosh looked as if she didn't know what to do.

"You won't, Zosh. We need you. Please. Just hang on to the saddle and go as fast as you can. If you get scared, pull back on the reins. Dolly will slow down. I promise." Beth ran to the mare and put the reins back over her neck. "Come on. Quick, Zosh."

Zosh was trembling as she tried to throw her leg over Dolly's back, and Beth steadied her. "If you see anyone coming, hide," Beth instructed. "Don't let them see you. Then get Mrs. Wentworth and the police."

"I'll . . . I'll try my best," Zosh said.

"You'll make it," Beth encouraged.

Beth watched Zosh bounce off down the path at a slow trot. "Hang on," she called. Then she started pulling at the door again. She could have cried in frustration: she wasn't getting anywhere.

She went back around to the window. Now that Zosh was gone, she was beginning to feel nervous. She hoped help would come soon. She was a little afraid of Mr. Carl. If he showed up, while she was alone . . .

The window was hooked inside. Beth carefully put her hand through the broken pane and reached for the hook. It was rusty and corroded, so she had a hard time freeing it from the eye. Finally it came loose. She nicked her wrist pulling her hand back out. Charmin' whinnied. It was almost as if he were sympathizing with her. "I'm coming in, boy," she said, pushing against the window. It gave, and she was able to get it open enough to get her leg and arm in and squeeze through. She scratched her thigh on one of the old boards. "Ouch!" she said, but she was inside. She put her arms around the horse's neck. "Oh, Charmin'," she said, "I was so worried about you." She was dirty and sweaty and frightened. "Who put you here, feller?" she said.

The shed had a dirt floor. It was gloomy and dark. She made out a water bucket and some remnants of hay. "At least they fed you." She went over to the door and threw her body against it. Maybe she could push it loose from the inside. All she wanted was to get Charmin' out, to get herself out, to be away from here. She thought she felt it move a little, so she backed up and threw herself against it again. Charmin' shied nervously. "It's all right," she told him. "I'm going to help you." The hinge screeched like nails on a blackboard. She put both hands against the door and strained. She could hear it giving. She took a deep breath; she had to rest a minute.

She had an idea and led the horse over to the door. "Knock on it," she said, "like you do at the barn. Knock on it." She tried to lift Charmin's leg. He pulled back, his head up, snorting. "I'm sorry, Charmin'," Beth said. "I must be freaking out." She went back, straining once more with her body against the door.

Then she heard a sound. She couldn't be sure, but it sounded like a car motor. Could Zosh have brought the police already? No—an ordinary car couldn't get down the old logging trail. It would scrape on the bottom. Who, then? She crept over to the window that faced the path, crouched down so she wouldn't be seen, and peered out. There wasn't anyone there. She started to sigh with relief, then heard voices. She knelt, frozen.

She could see a patch of blue coming through the bushes, and something dark behind it. She almost cried out for joy. It was Dave! She started to call to him, but stopped. There was a man behind him, a man she'd never seen before. Dave stumbled forward. The man had pushed him! He caught up to Dave and shoved him again.

"Lay off, will you." Dave's voice sounded high, thin.

"Just move, kid." The man punched Dave in the shoulder.

Dave grimaced in pain, grabbing his shoulder where he had been hit. "I brought you here, didn't I? You don't have to get rough."

"This is nothing." Beth saw an ugly smile on the man's face. He reached up and pushed back lank, dark hair.

Something in his other hand caught the light. It was a gun.

CHAPTER 13

Dave didn't even sound like himself, and that frightened Beth almost as much as the man with the gun.

"Open up that shed," the man ordered.

"Look," Dave was pleading, "can't we just leave him here? I'll get him out of the country. Curtis and I have it all planned. He's made arrangements to have the horse shipped from New York to Mexico. I'm expecting him here anytime—"

"Your friend Curtis is in the hospital. A little case of broken ribs." He pushed the gun into Dave's back. "How do you think we found you after Joe Carl put out the word something funny was going on up here?"

"The hospital?" Beth could hear Dave suck in his breath. "Bad?"

"He'll live. Now, you think it might be a good idea to

do as you're told? Get that shed open and move that horse out."

"But if you kill him and get caught . . ."

"I won't get caught. I'm getting rid of him before anyone starts looking."

Oh, no! Beth felt her throat tighten. He was talking about Charmin'!

"They've probably missed him already," Dave said. "But no one will look for him here. Can't you just—"

"You screwed up, kid," the man snarled. "Gallant Ruler should've been horsemeat months ago. Now, if I were you, I wouldn't want to add any more insult to injury. Do as you're told, and you might come out of this with your hide. It may not look as pretty as it does now, but at least it'll be in one piece. Open that door!"

How could Dave be mixed up with this man, Beth thought, trembling. And what had he said about a gallant ruler? Maybe she was too scared for it to make sense. The man gave Dave a push, and he almost fell right into the window. They were so close, she could see the hard metal of the gun shining in the sun. Beth flattened herself on the ground.

She heard them move around to the shed door. Now was her chance to climb out the window and run. She got to her feet, but she knew she couldn't leave Dave and Charmin'.

Oh, Zosh, she prayed, Zosh, please hurry. Get to Mrs. Wentworth's. Don't fall off. She felt as if all her energy were concentrated on getting Zosh there . . . helping by mental telepathy. She squeezed her eyes together and concentrated. Hurry, Zosh. We're in bad trouble.

"Stop stalling!" the man hollered.

"I'm trying to get it open," Dave protested.

There was the sound of metal on metal, and then Beth, her mouth open and her hand at her throat, watched the door swing inward.

Dave stepped through it. "Beth!" He looked at her in amazement.

Behind him, the gunman peered over his shoulder. "What the—!"

"Beth, how did you . . . ?"

"What is this?" The man jammed his gun into Dave's back. "Another double cross? Who's this kid?"

"She's the girl who rode Gallant Ruler," Dave said, staring at Beth. "But what are you doing here? How did you—"

"Don't play dumb. You knew she was here. Probably thought I wouldn't do it if there was a witness. You know what, kid, you're just too big for your breeches. But it ain't going to work. All it means is, now I got two of you to persuade that silence is golden. Right, girl?" He grabbed Beth's arm and twisted it roughly. "He planted you here, didn't he?"

"No!" Beth cried out in pain. "No. Let me go, please. You're hurting me."

"When you talk." He kept a painful pressure on her arm. "Tell me your boyfriend planned this."

"He didn't!" Beth howled. "Please, let go!"

"Let her go." Dave started to move closer but found

a gun in his face. "How could I have planned it? I didn't know you were in town. You found me and made me bring you here. How could I have gotten in touch with her?"

The man released Beth's arm and shoved her toward the wall. "Put your hands up and don't try to get away."

Beth staggered back, crying and rubbing her limp arm. It felt lifeless.

"How many other people know where this nag is?" The man glared at Dave.

"No one else knows. Beth didn't know. I didn't tell her."

"How'd you get here?" His face came close to hers. His breath smelled bad, and she felt nauseous.

"I was . . . looking for Charmin'. I found the fence down and followed the path. I thought he'd gotten out by himself." Beth looked at Dave. "I don't understand," she wept.

"I didn't mean to get you into this, Beth." Dave looked as if he were going to cry, too.

"Well, she's in it."

The loud voices and the tension in the air seemed to affect Charmin'. He whirled around abruptly and headed for the door. The gunman backed up but kept his gun on Dave. "Grab him!" he ordered. Dave reached up and caught Charmin's halter. "Take him outside. And you"—he waved the gun at Beth—"walk right behind him."

It was a nightmare, and she couldn't wake up. Numb, she followed along behind Charmin'.

"Take him out to the trailer," the man ordered. He was behind Beth, keeping a good distance from the horse.

Beth's heart began to pound. Then he wasn't going to shoot Charmin' here. If that was true, maybe they had a chance to save him.

"Where are we going?" Beth's voice was small.

"Your boyfriend is taking us way back in the woods. He'd better not be lying about an old abandoned gravel pit there," he snarled. "Keep moving!"

At the top of the path was the Fuller Jeep hitched to a horse trailer. "You go hold the horse," he said, pointing the gun at Beth. She did as she was told.

"You get this rig turned around," he told Dave. "And don't get funny, or this thing's liable to go off, and she'll get hurt."

Dave pulled the Jeep into the path, but there wasn't room to maneuver the trailer, too. "Unhitch it," the man ordered. Beth wondered what would happen if she ran. He would probably shoot her. Maybe he was going to anyway.

Oh, Dave, go slow. Go slow, she prayed to herself. Help is on the way.

Dave seemed to sense her thoughts. He fiddled with the hitch until the gunman got impatient and started threatening him. Then he crashed around in the brush getting the trailer turned around.

Why didn't someone come? It had been a long time. Beth pictured Zosh lying unconscious after a bad fall. She should have gone with her. Zosh had asked her to come. Why did she always have to be such a know-it-all?

"Get the horse in," the man said to Beth.

Dave opened the doors and let the ramp down. Beth started to reach in her pocket for the sugar she always carried; then she stopped herself. It was worth a chance. Charmin' hated to be pulled. If she yanked him hard enough, maybe . . .

"Move it!"

She walked Charmin' over to the ramp and tugged on his halter. He threw his head up and pulled back, taking her with him. "Stop that!" she screamed, hoping to upset him further.

"Help her get him in," the man told Dave.

Dave moved around behind the horse. He gave him a slap on the rump just as Beth jerked down. Charmin' reared and twisted to the side, tearing the halter out of Beth's hands. He plunged and kicked, then galloped off down the path.

"Get him!" the man yelled.

They started running down the path, but as Charmin' disappeared around a bend they heard a voice cry, "Whoa! Whoa!" Then a man came into view.

"What the—" their captor exclaimed angrily.

"It's the sheriff!" Dave shouted.

The gunman glared at him, then turned and ran the other way.

Beth tore down the path toward safety, Dave keeping pace right beside her.

"What's going on here?" The sheriff jogged up to meet them. "Got this wild story 'bout a stolen hoss from the youngster back there." Beth could have screamed with joy. Zosh was coming up the path, and behind her was Mr. Fuller, leading Charmin'.

"You want that man. He's got a gun," Beth heard Dave say as she threw her arms around Zosh.

"You saved our lives!" She was sobbing uncontrollably.

"Where's this man you're talking about?" the sheriff asked.

Dave pointed. "He took off—that way. But be careful."

"That's the dangedest thing I ever heard," the sheriff said. "Now, you want to just calm down and tell me what this is all about?"

"You're going to need help. I'm telling you he's dangerous," Dave insisted.

The sheriff gave him a hard stare. "All right, Dave, you come with me," he finally said.

Dave and the sheriff ran off in the direction the gunman had taken.

"Mr. Fuller," Beth cried, "you shouldn't have let Dave go. That man could kill him!"

"Didn't have much choice." Percy's mouth was pursed, and the lines on his forehead deepened. "Let's load up Charmin' and get back to the house. I'm going to call the troopers."

It was slow going down the rutted path, and Beth kept looking out the window apprehensively, peering into the woods, afraid he might be hiding there, waiting to ambush them. Percy questioned her about what she had seen at the shed. She stammered and repeated herself as she tried to describe it. Things were going around in her head faster than they could come out of her mouth.

"Now, just you wind down, Beth. Take one thing at a time," Percy said. "This fella had a gun and was threatening you and Dave?"

"He was talking about a double cross and pushing Dave around—kicking, hitting—it was awful. He wanted to kill Charmin'. Maybe us. Talking about a gallant ruler. I pulled on Charmin'. He ran away, and then you came."

"Beth, look at your arm!" Zosh stared wide-eyed at the ugly purple bruises.

"He twisted it. I thought he was going to break it."

"I'll just have a look at it when we get to the house," Percy said.

"He was going to take us to a gravel pit. He was going to shoot Charmin'. I heard him say so." Beth began to cry, the fear flooding over her as she remembered.

Zosh put her arm around her. "Oh, poor Beth," she said, her voice trembling.

"Don't sound like the sheriff and Dave's enough to handle that fella if they do find him," Percy said as they pulled onto the road and he gunned the engine. "I'll call from the camp. Then I'd better run you over to Doc Slater's. Seems like you could use something to calm you down."

The Jeep roared down the road until Percy screeched to a halt in front of his house. With one quick movement he had the door open and was on his way in.

"Do you want me to get you some water?" Zosh asked.

Beth couldn't seem to stop sobbing. She swallowed hard and nodded.

Percy was right behind Zosh as she came out with a glass in hand.

"Got the state troopers," he said. "They'll get him. I'll just unload Charmin', and we'll run on over to Doc's."

Beth took sips of the water. Finally she was able to tell him. "Please," she said. "I don't want to go. Please. Can't we just wait here for Dave?"

"Well . . ." Percy looked uncertain. "Don't want you faintin' or gettin' sick. . . ."

Beth took a deep breath. "I'm all right. I was just . . . just scared. But now we're here. I'm okay. I couldn't go anywhere . . . I couldn't . . . not knowing . . . Dave . . ."

"All right." Percy reached in and gently lifted her arm. "I reckon I know how you feel. I'm kinda bol-luxed, too. You just lean on me, and we'll tend to you here." He put her arm around his shoulder and lifted her out of the Jeep.

Beth leaned on him gratefully. Her knees felt weak. "Where's Dolly?" she suddenly asked.

"I left her at Mrs. Wentworth's. She was going to take her back to the farm," Zosh said.

"You want to lie down a bit?" Percy asked as they went into the house.

"I couldn't," Beth said.

"Well, then." He led her into the kitchen. "You just set here in the rocker. Rockin's awful soothin'."

When she was calm, and Percy had examined her arm and found nothing broken, he asked her to go over the story again. Once she had finished, Percy said, "Well, we know the 'what' of it, Beth, but we don't know the 'why' of it." He glanced for about the twentieth time at the old clock on the mantel. "Sure don't sound like the kind of character my boy should have any truck with. His mother's going to have a fit when she gets home and hears about it."

"Mother!" Beth said. "I don't know what I'm thinking of. I should have called my parents! They'll be worried about us."

She told them very little over the phone, but they wanted to come right down and get her and Zosh. "It's been an hour," Beth begged. "Please, Dave's got to come soon. Please, let me wait. I'll call you when he does."

Percy got on the phone to assure them that Beth was all right and in good hands. While he was talking, a car pulled into the driveway. Beth ran to the screen door. "It's Dave!"

She heard the sheriff call to Dave as he came up the path, "Might have to take you in later, Dave."

Dave nodded, his head down.

"Did you get that man?" Beth could hardly contain herself.

"No," Dave said, "but the troopers are out. We heard it on the sheriff's radio."

Percy put down the phone. He started forward as if to embrace him, then stopped. "You're white as a sheet, son."

"Yeah." Dave slumped into the kitchen rocker.

" 'Pears like you got a story to tell us."

"You're not going to like it, Dad." Dave didn't look at his father.

"Maybe we ought to leave, Zosh," Beth said reluctantly.

"No, Beth." Dave swallowed. "You're owed an explanation, too. Don't imagine you'll want to see me anymore, anyway."

"Might as well get it off your chest, Dave," his father said.

"I didn't win Charmin' on a bet," Dave began.

"Uh-huh." Percy nodded. "That was kinda hard to swallow, a horse like that. But you never been a liar, Dave. Musta had a reason."

"Not one you'll be proud of. I got in trouble. Me and Curtis. Dad, it's so hard to explain. You haven't been to Virginia. You don't know what it's like. You hear about people being on the 'fast track.' Well, I'll tell you, the fast track is the racetrack."

"I'm not following . . ." Percy said.

"I got in over my head. Curtis is part of this crowd—well, not really part of it. I'm not blaming him. See, he didn't realize either . . ."

"Why don't you just start at the beginning and tell us what happened?" Percy said.

"You know how against racing I've been since I got home, but I wasn't down South—not at first I wasn't. It was exciting. There was a lot of money changing hands. I guess I knew from the beginning it wasn't exactly legal. . . ."

"You trying to tell me you got mixed up with crooks?"

Dave was silent a moment, then nodded. "That's what they are, all right—and worse, but I didn't know it. I swear I didn't. I thought it was very big-time stuff . . . very sophisticated. Dad, the first time I bet, I won a thousand dollars!"

"That's a lot of money, Dave, but I'm going to give you odds, you didn't keep winning like that."

"You're right. Oh, I'd win sometimes, but I lost a lot. And then I lost more. Curtis and I hit a losing streak at the same time. That's when we started doing favors for these guys. . . ."

"Those gamblers?" Percy frowned.

"I know. We should have known better. But it didn't seem like much at the time, and we wanted to keep on the right side of them. We delivered money, messages, nothing heavy."

"Not heavy, but illegal?" Percy voiced Beth's

thought. It was hard to believe Dave had been taken in by criminals.

"Right again, Dad. We were on the wrong side of the law and really, really in debt."

"How much?"

"I don't even want to tell you." He swallowed. "Close to thirty thousand between the two of us."

"Lord have mercy, Dave!" Percy's face had lost its color.

"Thirty thousand dollars!" Beth exclaimed.

"They really had us. What can I tell you? By then we knew what fools we'd been, but it was too late. They started putting pressure on us to pay the money. Told Curtis to get it from his father."

"But his father wouldn't deal with mobsters," Percy suggested.

"Not that exactly. The Eatons have a fancy place— you know, like *Gone With the Wind*—the long driveway, stables, big pretty white house, but it turns out everything's mortgaged to the hilt. Racehorses are expensive, and they've had some bad luck. So Curtis's father couldn't help even if he would have."

What a terrible story, Beth thought. It was as if the boys had been trapped.

"What'd you do then, Dave? I got an awful feeling we're getting to the worst part of this terrible tale."

Dave looked down at the ground. "Yes. I guess it was Mr. Eaton they were after all along. They twisted Curtis's arm, and I mean that literally. He set up a meeting with his father."

"To do what?" Zosh voiced their confusion.

"Some horse trading. Some horse trading that would make this group a bunch of money."

"Spell it out, Dave," Percy said.

"The Eatons had a horse—Gallant Ruler—who was supposed to run in the Florida Stakes. The horse had a good crack at it."

"Gallant Ruler!" Percy exclaimed. "I knew that name was familiar. That's the horse that was supposed to be a Derby contender, but went bad. Started losing all his races."

"That's what you think. That's what this crowd wanted you to think. You and the rest of the racing world. They persuaded Mr. Eaton to run a look-alike, who only had to be touched up a little to pass as Gallant Ruler. The two horses had the same sire, and the brood mares were sisters—so—the same bloodlines. But one could run and the other couldn't."

"Why did Curtis's father agree? To save you boys?"

"Partly, I guess. These guys are smooth, Dad. They offered him a wonderful deal—a lot of money he needed badly, the write-off of our debts. They even threw in a promising colt. He got taken just like we did."

"Makes me sick." Percy scratched his head and sighed. "There he is with a winning horse, and he cheats and doesn't run it. I reckon we know now why you brought home a horse."

"You don't know all of it."

Beth held her breath. She had figured out that Charmin' was Gallant Ruler and that Gallant Ruler had been brought to New Hampshire so he would not be seen. Her mind had been racing. No wonder Dave hadn't wanted him in the race or in the paper!

"They had promised Mr. Eaton when he shipped the other horse to Florida that Gallant Ruler would be hidden out, used for stud. But they either were lying or changed their minds. They'd won a lot of money by running horses against the fake Gallant Ruler. They decided it wasn't safe. They told him to destroy the horse and deliver its body to a hacker."

"A hacker?" Beth was almost afraid to hear the answer.

"He'd be cut up for dog food," Dave said dully.

Beth gagged, and Zosh looked ill.

"It's disgusting, and I don't know what they did to convince him, but they must have threatened him with something unspeakable. I don't think he would have gone along just on the basis of blackmail . . . though he would be ruined if the racing commission got a whiff of what he'd done. Anyway, he put it on Curtis."

"But Curtis couldn't do it!" Beth exclaimed.

"Neither of us could, Beth. We've grown up taking care of animals, not killing them. We touched up his color. Made him darker—shortened his blaze. We got the Eatons' trainer in on it. He'd gone along with the substitution out of loyalty, but he'd hated it. We knew he'd help us save the horse. And he did. He came up with a horse that had died on a neighbor's farm and sent him to the hacker's instead. We brought Gallant

Ruler home. I was only to keep him until Curtis or the trainer could make arrangements to ship him to Mexico or South America. Nobody would have been the wiser, but then you entered him in the race. . . ."

Now it all made sense to Beth: Dave's moods; his anger; his fury at the newspapermen. She didn't know whether to be proud of him or frightened for him. "You took a chance," she said, "going against criminals like that!"

"Don't know if I'd compliment him, Beth." Percy's mouth was tight, and he looked gray under his tan. "He ain't exactly free of blame in this. Son, you coulda got yourself killed. I'm not sayin' your savin' the horse wasn't a fine thing. It was. But you shouldn't have been involved in the first place. How you ever let yourself get mixed up with criminals just beats me. I'll never understand it."

"I guess you won't. All I can say is, I wish it had never happened."

"And you been lying to me all summer, Dave. I can't get over it. And how's your mother going to feel? Hm? She sets a lot of store by you."

"I'm sorry. I am going to try to make it up to you. I hated lying. I hated myself."

Beth and Zosh were embarrassed. They didn't belong in this family scene. Beth got up, and Zosh quickly followed.

"I'd better get home," Beth said. "My parents are worried."

"You can ride Charmin' home if you want, Beth,"

Dave said. "I don't know what's going to happen to him, but for today he's yours. You helped save his life."

Beth could feel a lump in her throat and the tears trying to come into her eyes. "Okay," she managed to say.

"Maybe I could borrow a horse? A gentle one?" Zosh asked, obviously pleased with herself.

Beth tried to smile. At least one good thing had come out of the day. Dave went to the barn with them to pick out the horse. Beth forced herself to ask the question she had been dreading to ask. "I've got to know something, Dave," she said as they were saddling the horses. "Did they find Charmin' . . . Gallant Ruler"—the name still sounded weird to her—"because of . . . my picture in the paper?"

"That was only part of it," he said. "Remember the guy named Carl at the racetrack?"

"Of course. Was he in on this, too?"

"Not the original scheme, no. But he got suspicious. He was timing some of your workouts. He sent his trainer to the barn early one morning, but you came in and he ducked out. Carl and the trainer came back later that day. He took some turpentine, and some dye came off. So he started making inquiries . . . put the word out. I think he thought, once he couldn't beat you in that race, that he'd scare me into selling him the horse. He wanted to know what he was buying. Anyway, his connections had connections, and the original group got wind of this mystery horse. Then the picture hit the papers. They got to Curtis. He admitted it was Gallant Ruler, so they sent that goon up here. . . ."

"I could kill myself!" Beth said.

"It wasn't your fault." Zosh leaped to her defense. "How did you know it was a stolen horse?"

"I should have listened to you, Dave." Beth didn't want his feelings hurt by what Zosh had said. He hadn't meant to do anything bad either.

"No you shouldn't. I screwed up from the beginning, and I just kept making things worse and worse. Once the story hit the papers, I thought I could hide the horse—let him quietly disappear until Curtis could get him into Mexico. Every time I should have told the truth I didn't. Instead, I tricked you and your family into going to the Rebekahs' dinner to get you out of the way while I took Charmin'. Then the goon shows up and makes me take him to the horse. I'm sorry. I didn't know you were there, but that's no excuse. I could have gotten us both hurt badly."

There was nothing to say. It was all true. Beth knew now how his father felt. He had lied to his family, and he had tricked her. That really hurt. She had thought he had wanted to spend the evening with her, but he had just wanted to keep them away from the farm so he could take Charmin'. She led the horse out of the barn without a word.

Outside, Dave helped Zosh to mount. "Thank you," she muttered, not looking at him.

Dave hesitated, then walked over to Charmin' and reached for Beth's arm. She flinched. He dropped his hand as if he'd been burned. "Don't even want me to touch you?" he asked.

"That's my sore arm. Where he twisted it," Beth said through tight lips.

"I said you wouldn't want to see me again. I was right, huh?" He didn't move away.

"Why would you want to see me, anyway?" Beth asked. "You're not planning to steal the horse again, are you? You won't need to get me out of the way again, will you?" She couldn't help the bitter words.

"I guess I had that coming," Dave said, looking up at her steadily, "but you know that's not it. You know . . . well, Beth . . . you know how I feel about you."

"No, I don't," she said stubbornly.

"Well, if I don't go to jail—and if you let me—I'll come and tell you." He turned and walked toward the house.

Percy appeared at the door. He was almost smiling. "They got him," he called, looking only at Dave. "They got the fella."

It was the first day of school. Beth was excited and a little bit scared. Compared to junior high, Riverdale High School was enormous. Like all the other entering sophomores, she was sure she would never find her way around.

There was no one else at her bus stop. It would have been nice to have someone to talk to while she waited. She pulled the Manchester newspaper out of her book bag and read the front-page story for about the tenth time.

LOCAL BOY TO TESTIFY. That was the headline. "David Fuller, 19, of Pumpkin Hill Road, will give evidence before a grand jury in Richmond, Virginia, on September 5."

Dave. Just thinking about him, she felt her face grow warm and her hands begin to tingle. The day before yesterday still seemed like a dream. She had been reading and hadn't wanted to go to the door when the bell rang. Going through the dining room, she had glanced out the window. His Jeep had been parked out front. Like a ninny, she'd stood and stared at it, not believing what she was seeing. The bell had rung again, and her mother had yelled, "For heaven's sake, Beth, will you answer that door!"

It couldn't be. That's all she could think as she had moved in a daze to the front hall. Then she opened the front door, and there he was. He was wearing khakis and a white T-shirt. She had stood and stared at him.

"Hi," he'd said, grinning at her.

No words would come out of her mouth. She must have looked like an idiot, just standing there.

"Can I come in?" he asked.

She moved back. "Sure. I mean, of course you can."

"You still mad?"

She had managed to shake her head from side to side. She couldn't believe it was Dave. He was standing in her house. She had thought she would never see him again.

"I was going to write you," he said, "but everything was up in the air. Dad had to get a lawyer. It looked for a while like I might have to go to jail. I didn't think you'd want to hear from a jailie."

"I've been worried," she managed to say.

"I figured. But things have worked out. Sort of."

"Who is it, Beth?" She could hear her mother coming from the kitchen. "Why, Dave Fuller! How nice to see you!" Her mother smiled tentatively. "Come on out on the patio. We're dying for news."

Once they were settled with lemonade, Dave told them he was on his way to Virginia to testify before the grand jury.

"We've all been just sick over you, Dave," Elinor Bridgewater said, "especially Beth. It was a shame we had to leave when we did. It's hard on people when things are unresolved. I've called your dad a few times, but . . . issues were still in doubt."

"Mother!" Beth gave her a warning look. Sometimes her mother just didn't know when to stop talking.

"It didn't look so hot for a while," Dave said, "but my parents really stood behind me."

"Now what happens in Virginia?" Elinor asked.

"This is kind of a weird case, I guess. The grand jury will decide what indictments should be brought. Because we're cooperating, there won't be any charges against Curtis or me."

"Oh, Dave, that's wonderful!" Beth said.

"Better'n I deserve, that's for sure. They've got that man, Beth. What they're holding him on is attempted robbery with a dangerous weapon. He's refused to talk."

"What will happen to Curtis's father?" asked Beth.

"Mr. Eaton has fancy lawyers who'll do what's called plea bargaining. He may go to jail, though—and he'll certainly never breed horses again. I brought you a copy of the Manchester paper. It explains the whole thing."

"But you'll be able to go back to school?" Elinor asked.

"Not exactly, Mrs. Bridgewater." Dave looked embarrassed. "I didn't do well last year. My head wasn't exactly straight . . . about a lot of things. My dad thinks it would be a good idea if I stayed around home and worked for a year before I go back."

"Punishment?" Beth said sympathetically.

"Consequences." Dave smiled and winked at her. He imitated his father's drawl, affectionately rather than bitterly. "Ayeh, there are consequences for youah acshuns."

"You don't seem unhappy about it," Elinor said.

"I guess I'm still enough of a Yankee to recognize that particular brand of New England justice," Dave answered.

"Sounds to me as if you have your head straight and your values too." Elinor smiled.

"What about Charmin'?" Beth said softly. It hurt to ask about him. She missed him so much.

"He's in Dad's custody. After the grand jury hands down an indictment, he'll be returned to Virginia." Dave smiled at her. "Curtis tells me their trainer is going to buy him. He'll be in good hands."

"I'll never see him again," Beth said quietly.

"Sure you will. I thought maybe you'd come up and visit for a fall weekend before he goes. I'll drive down and get you."

She didn't know how to respond. He was asking her up for a whole weekend!

"Do you want to?" he said, sounding a little unsure.

"I'd love to!" The words came out louder than she intended.

"When do you have to be in Virginia, Dave?" her mother asked.

"Day after tomorrow," he told her.

"Then you must spend the night with us." Elinor got up. "I'd better go in and do something about dinner," she said.

Dave reached over and squeezed Beth's hand once her mother had gone inside. "It only takes four hours to get here from New Hampshire. It takes eight from Virginia. I'm not sorry I'll be closer."

He liked her. There could be no mistaking it.

"I'm glad," she'd said.

Beth could see the bus rounding the corner and she quickly stuffed the newspaper into her book bag. She'd almost forgotten where she was and resented the bus's interrupting her reliving of the time spent with Dave.

Its brakes protested loudly as the bus cranked to a stop. Lights flashed and the stop sign swung out as the door opened to admit her.

"Beth! Beth!" Tory was waving frantically and pointing to the empty seat beside her about halfway back in the bus.

The aisle was narrow, and Beth lurched against a body half out of a crowded seat as she made her way back.

"I saved you a seat," Tory said, picking up a shiny new blue notebook. "We've all been dying to see you. When did you get back from hicksville?"

Beth decided to ignore the insult to her beloved New Hampshire. "Two weeks ago," she said. "I tried to get hold of you guys, but no one ever answered the phone. I figured you were all away on vacation."

"We were," Tory said, "but everyone was back by Saturday. You should have called again."

"Yeah." Actually Beth had not been sorry to find the gang out of town. It would have made it hard to see Zosh if they'd been around. She had been so worried about Dave, and Zosh was the only one who could understand. They'd talked about the summer endlessly until Zosh and her father had gone to Buffalo for Labor Day weekend. She could hardly wait to tell her about Dave's visit.

"Boy, I'll bet you're glad to be back," Tory said. "Amy said it was really dead up there."

"What have you guys been doing?" Beth changed the subject. Dead, she thought. She'd won a horse race, helped catch a gangster. . . . That's what Dave had said. It was obvious her group didn't even read the papers. There had been a story in *The New York Times*.

". . . and you missed a great party Saturday. We took a keg to the beach. You should have seen Darlene. . . ."

Beth realized she hadn't heard half of what Tory was saying. She didn't care. She tuned her out again.

At ten this morning, Dave would be before the grand jury. He'd promised to call her tonight and to stop on his way back. They had sat together on the terrace after her parents had gone in to watch the late news. That's when he said he would call her. Then he'd looked at her funny, and she knew he was going to kiss her. Her nose had felt too big, like it was in the way, and she couldn't get any air. Finally he had let her go. She was afraid she hadn't kissed him right, but he had held on to her hand, and said, "I've been thinking about doing that almost all summer."

She smiled at him. "Me too," she managed.

"Then we'd better do it again. This time for you."

It was better this time. She didn't feel like she was running out of breath. "Hey," he'd said, fooling with her hair. "Do you know, when I first saw you, I thought you were a little kid." I was, she thought, and a spoiled brat at that.

Tory punched her arm. "Are you listening?"

"Sorry. What did you say?" Beth asked.

"I said we're all supposed to meet on the circle in front of the glass corridor. Then Amy'll show us where to sit in the student center. She's got it all figured out."

Beth had heard about the student center. It served as both cafeteria and social meeting place for the high school. It was huge—the size of a couple of football fields. Some sections were considered "in" and others considered "out." That seemed kind of silly to her, but still . . . it wouldn't hurt to sit in the right place.

"Come on." Tory pushed her as she stood up. Nobody wanted to wait, and there was a lot of shoving as they got off the bus.

They found Amy and Darlene by the entrance door to the glass corridor. The corridor connected the huge main building with the music and gym wing. "Isn't this neat," Amy said as they made their way to the center. "No more dumb hall passes. We can go where we want when we want."

"Except when we have classes," Darlene said.

"Oh, you can get around that, too." Amy laughed.

Just like Amy, Beth thought. She'd always find a way to beat the system.

"We're going to sit over there." Amy pointed to a group of tables in front of a large square enclosure in the middle of the enormous room. "That's where the jocks sit."

"Hey, Amy!" A blond curly-haired boy waved them over. "Come and join us." There were two other boys at the table and only three seats. Beth hung back as the others sat down. "Come on, Beth," Amy said.

"It's okay. I'll stand," Beth answered.

"Don't be dumb," Amy said. "There's room, isn't there, guys? Especially for my best friend."

"Sure." The blond boy leaned back and pulled up a chair from another table.

Beth sat down. Amy introduced her to the boys. Everyone else knew one another.

"You look better than you did on Saturday night," one of the boys teased Darlene.

"Oh, hang it up," she said. "You were wasted yourself."

Everybody started arguing about who had more to

drink on Saturday night. Beth wondered if Zosh had gotten to school yet. She looked around the room, but it was too big. She probably couldn't spot her even if she were there. Their homerooms were next to each other. They'd compared assignments when they had come in the mail last week. Zosh would probably go right to her room rather than come to the center alone.

Beth got up. "Where're you going?" Amy asked.

"I'll be back," Beth said, not answering.

She was halfway across the room when she saw Zosh coming through the door from the corridor. She hurried toward her. Zosh saw her and waved. Beth reached in her bag and pulled out the Manchester paper.

"Dave was here!" Beth exulted as they met and squeezed each other's hands. "Wait till I tell you!"

"What's all this?"

Beth turned around, surprised. Amy was right behind her. "Is that the hunk I met in New Hampshire?"

"Yeah." Beth had planned to tell Amy the story, but that table full of jocks didn't seem the place. She handed Zosh the paper. "It's on the front page," she said.

"So what was Dave doing here? Does he have the hots for you?" Amy was all interest.

Beth felt her face get red. It was a term she'd used herself. Before she knew what it felt like to . . . feel the way she did about Dave. Whatever she felt, it certainly wasn't anything as crude as "the hots."

"No," she said. "See, this wild thing happened. . . ."

Beth told her about the race and the man who had tried to kill Charmin'.

"It sounds just like Nancy Drew." Amy laughed, belittling the story. "Let's go back to the table."

"Not now. I want to talk to Zosh."

"Zosh?" Amy looked puzzled.

"Sophie," Beth said quietly. "That's her nickname."

Amy looked at Zosh. "That's a funny name," she said. "I've never heard it before."

"It's Polish," Zosh said.

"Oh." Amy smiled. "You've lost some more weight, haven't you . . . Zash?" She deliberately mispronounced it. "And you're wearing your hair down. Looks great. You're a regular Farrah Fawcett."

Beth felt like strangling her. She saw Zosh's shoulders slump. She was staring at the floor, looking awkward and embarrassed. It was almost as if Amy had pushed a button and poor out-of-place Sophie was reappearing.

"Let's go," Amy said to Beth. "You can talk to her later."

Beth hesitated. It was a big school. With Amy, she was sure to be in. Without her, she'd be taking her chances.

"Go ahead, Beth."

Beth looked at Zosh, who managed a smile.

"I'd rather talk to you. I'll see Amy another time," Beth said.

"Don't hold your breath until the time comes." Amy turned away angrily.

It was a big school, but she'd be all right, Beth realized. She had Dave, and she had Zosh, and she had herself. She didn't need Amy.

She linked her arm through Zosh's. "Let's find a table," she said, "away from the jocks."